ZANE PRE

The AFTERMATH

SHELIA M. GOSS

Dear Reader:

Keeping up with the Joneses is not always what it seems. Sometimes it can be mysterious involving a web of intrigue and suspense. Such is the case with *The Aftermath*, the sequel to *The Joneses*, named by *Library Journal* as one of the best books of 2014.

While continuing to operate the Louisiana-based RJ Jones Funeral Home, family members turn their focus on supporting patriarch Royce, who's imprisoned for the murder of his former best friend, Jason Milton, a businessman who later proved to be envious. Once viewed as the pillar of the community, Royce is now under the scrutiny of the public eye.

His wife, Lexi, and their children, Charity, Hope and Lovie, become relentless sleuths in their mission to prove Royce's innocence. Readers will experience a roller-coaster ride through prison visits and evidence collection that ends with a startling revelation. Secrets are unlocked and scandal is exposed at each turn in this Southern whodunit.

As always, thanks for the love and support shown to myself and the authors that I publish under Strebor Books. We appreciate each and every one of you and will continue to strive to bring you cutting-edge, exciting books in the future. For more information, please join my Facebook page @AuthorZane, Twitter @AuthorZane, or Instagram@ AuthorZane and visit me at Eroticanoir.com.

Blessings,

Zane

Publisher
Strebor Books
www.simonandschuster.com

ALSO BY SHELIA M. GOSS

The Joneses

ZANE PRESENTS

The AFTERMATH

SHELIA M. GOSS

SBI
STREBOR BOOKS
NEW YORK LONDON TORONTO SYDNEY

Strebor Books
P.O. Box 6505
Largo, MD 20792
http://www.streborbooks.com

ISBN 978-1-59309-620-5
ISBN 978-1-4767-8331-4 (ebook)
LCCN 2014942331

First Strebor Books trade paperback edition April 2015

Cover design: www.mariondesigns.com
Cover photograph: © Keith Saunders/Keith Saunders Photos

10 9 8 7 6 5 4 3 2 1

Manufactured in the United States of America

For information regarding special discounts for bulk purchases, please contact Simon & Schuster Special Sales at 1-866-506-1949 or business@simonandschuster.com

The Simon & Schuster Speakers Bureau can bring authors to your live event. For more information or to book an event, contact the Simon & Schuster Speakers Bureau at 1-866-248-3049 or visit our website at www.simonspeakers.com.

ACKNOWLEDGMENTS

This book is dedicated to the memory of my father, Lloyd Goss (1947-1996).

I'm grateful to God for allowing me another opportunity to do what I love doing.

I'm grateful for my mom, because without her support, I don't know where I would be.

I'm grateful to Zane for welcoming me into the Strebor Books family.

I'm grateful to Charmaine Parker for her patience.

I'm grateful to Dr. Maxine Thompson for her encouraging words.

I'm grateful to everyone's support as I ventured into new territories. I want to give a special shout-out to: Michelle Monkou, Lawanna Johnson, Carla Curtis, Stacy Deanne, Kandie Delley, Paulara Hawkins, Peggy Love, Sheila L. Jackson, Tina McKinney, Barbara Morgan, Shantal Young, Lasheera Lee, Kim Knight, Angelia Menchan, Ella Curry, Debra Owsley, Yolanda Gore, Lisa Borders Muhammad, Janice Ross, Michelle Lindo-Rice, LaShaunda Hoffman, Makasha Dorsey, Bettye Griffin, Melissa Love, Chrystal Dorsey, Kimyatta Walker, Paulette Harper-Johnson, Melesha Oglen, Renee Williams, Deatri King-Bey, Tamika Newhouse, Eboni Manning, Shelly Ellis, Teresa Beasley, Rhonda McKnight, the Agape Book Ministry in Richmond, VA and Building Relationships Around Books.

I'm grateful to all of you, the readers. There are so many of you so I can't list all of your names. Thank you _____ (fill in your name).

Shelia M. Goss

CHAPTER 1

Lexi

"Royce Jones, you've been found guilty of first-degree murder and sentenced to death under the state of Louisiana laws," the Shreveport, Louisiana judge said.

"Nooo!" I stood up to reach for my husband, Royce, but my knees buckled and I fell on the floor.

As soon as my body hit the floor, I woke up from my nightmare. I had fallen off the couch to the floor.

I guess I shouldn't have watched the news before drifting off to sleep. The media was having a field day with my husband's upcoming trial. How quickly people turn on you when you're faced with some adversities. Prior to Royce's arrest two months ago, people were singing Royce's praises, but now people were acting like they believe he killed Jason Milton. Jason was Royce's former best friend and according to news reports, he was also a prominent Shreveport businessman.

Royce had been the pillar of the community for the majority of his adult life, so I don't know why they would think he wasn't the same man they'd always known.

When Royce first got arrested for the murder of Jason, I wanted to crawl under the bed and not come out, but I couldn't. Royce needed me. My kids needed me. I had to be strong for Charity, Hope and Lovie. We had to pull together because the road ahead of us was rocky.

I eyed myself in the mirror one last time. I used extra makeup, hoping to hide the bags under my eyes from crying and lack of sleep. When I visited Royce, he needed to see a woman of strength. He needed to see in spite of the drama, I was still holding up. I didn't want him to see the strain of the situation on my face.

I eased my hand over my designer dress. I clasped on the pearls he'd once given me for an anniversary. I slipped on my heels and headed straight to the Caddo Correctional Center on the other side of Shreveport to visit my husband.

I was on autopilot because I barely remembered the drive from our house to the jail. I still didn't know why they couldn't have kept Royce at the city jail. I hated having to come here. I felt like I was having heart palpitations prior to each visit.

The officer at the front desk seemed to have an attitude every time I checked in at the visitors' window to see Royce. If she didn't like her job, she should've gotten another one. It was difficult enough to come see your loved one locked up; neither I nor any of the other people should've had to deal with her funky attitude.

I glanced around the room while I waited on Royce's name to be called. The visitation waiting room was filled with people of all races and economic backgrounds. Patience wasn't one of my strong points so I was glad when an officer called Royce's name.

I did a few breathing exercises as I walked down the long hall-way into cellblock C. I heard the clicks of the locks unlock and opened the door. There on the other side of the glass was my king, Royce, in a bright orange jumpsuit.

He watched me as I walked to the chair sitting opposite from his. Our hands went up to the glass. Unable to feel each other's hand because of the glass separating us, he picked up the phone on his side and I did the same. I wiped the black handle on my pants; I didn't know who had their ear up to the phone before me.

"Lexi, Baby, I'm so glad to see you," Royce said.

Something in the way he said it sent chills down my spine. I had to be strong.

"I'm glad to see you, too. I wish I could hug you." I ran my hand through my hair. I normally wore my hair shorter, but since Royce's arrest, I'd let my hair grow out.

"Me, too," he said.

"Baby, you're looking thin," was the next thing that blurted out of my mouth.

Royce wasn't a big man, but I was still used to seeing him with more weight on his six-foot-one frame.

"Lexi, the food isn't the greatest in here. I'm fine. I needed to lose some weight anyway. How are you? How are the kids?"

"I'm fine. I've just been worried about you."

"And the kids?" he asked again.

"They're hanging in there. You would be proud of Lovie. He's running things down at the funeral home so you don't have to worry about that."

"What about you? I can tell you're not sleeping."

"Royce, I'm fine. Don't worry about me."

"Easier said than done."

"The police are convinced that you murdered Jason. We know for a fact you didn't."

"Lexi, I've prayed about this. The truth will come out and then I will be a free man."

"It hasn't. You're not hearing what I'm hearing. If we leave it up to the police, they will have you on death row."

"It's not going to get to that."

Royce must have lost his mind while up in the prison. His delusional behavior about his situation was irking me.

"Royce, I've talked to our lawyers. They want you to plea bargain. They want you to admit to something you didn't do and get the charges down to second degree. Do you really want to spend years in prison? And with your age, it might as well be a death sentence because with as much time they will give you, you'll die in prison before you get out." My voice shook as I spoke.

"Calm down, baby. I'm trying to be optimistic."

"I understand that, but I have to be realistic. That's why I'm going to do my own investigation. I'm going to find out what really happened to Jason because dear, right now, all evidence points toward you. Thinking about killing someone and actually doing it are two different things. And I refuse to have you spend the rest of your life in prison for a crime you did not do."

Life is an illusion. One's perception determines their reception of the truth. I chose to believe that my husband, Royce Jones, will be proven innocent of the crime he's been accused of. With every breath I take, I will make sure of it.

CHAPTER 2

Royce

Once Lexi got an idea in her head to do something, she would not stop until she accomplished her goal. The reality of the situation was whoever killed Jason was still out there and I did not want her or my kids in harm's way. I would rather spend the rest of my days in jail if it would protect them from danger.

Seeing how outraged she was about my situation tugged at my heart.

"Lexi, calm down. You wanting to help mean the world to me, but you need to stay out of it."

"Stay out of it. How can I, Royce? If I sat back and did nothing, I wouldn't be able to live with myself."

"Promise me, you will be careful. Can you at least talk to Lovie about it? I will feel better if you let Lovie handle this. He knows people. He may be able to find out what happened. Or even talk to Charity's cop friend about it. Maybe he can help."

"I will talk to Lovie, but I don't trust the police right now, so talking to Charity's friend, well, let's just say I'll have to think long and hard on that before I do."

One of the guards walked up and tapped me on the shoulder.

I turned and looked back at Lexi. "Baby, time's up."

"Already? It seems like I just got here."

"I know. I'll see you next week," I said.

"I love you, Royce. I left a lot of money downstairs for you so please buy you something. In the past I complained about you eating junk food, but baby, you need to eat something."

"I'm eating," I assured her. "Take care of yourself."

"You too," Lexi replied.

"Baby, they called my name. I got to go. I love you," I said.

"I love you too."

Lexi blew me a kiss. I smiled. I got up and turned to walk away; I couldn't stand to see her walk away. I walked back to my cell. Normally, inmates had to share cells but because some of the guards knew me, or my family, they made sure I had a cell to myself.

I lay down on the bottom bunk and closed my eyes while tears crept out from the crevices of my lids. Even the strongest of men would cry under these circumstances. I tried to be strong for Lexi, but I really had no hope of ever getting out.

I also had spoken to our attorneys and the evidence they had against me would make any jury convict me. If I were on the jury, based on evidence alone, I would've convicted myself.

A part of me hoped Lexi wouldn't listen to me and would try to find out who really killed Jason. But that was selfish; the real killer seemed to have no empathy. They shot and killed Jason and then burned down his house to dispose of his body. If they did that, I didn't want to imagine what they would try to do to Lexi or the kids if they felt their identity would be exposed.

I'd had nothing but time on my hands. I sometimes felt like a caged animal. It could get cold and lonely behind those prison walls. I lay on the hard bed and stared at the ceiling. I closed my eyes as the vision of Lexi filled my thoughts. Lexi was a few inches shorter than me. Her feisty attitude was what originally attracted her to me.

I met her when Dad hired her to work at our family business, the RJ Jones Funeral Home. For me, it was love at first sight. Sure, I'd made mistakes along the way, but nothing could replace the love I had for Lexi.

One thought led to another. Since being locked up, my mind replayed my life over and over again. I'd replayed every event... every decision...and every scene in my life. I'd thought about the poor decisions I'd made that led me to this point. I thought about my friendship with Jason.

If I were being honest with myself, I could now see Jason for what he truly was. He was always looking for a get-rich scheme. He didn't always treat people fairly. Some of his business practices weren't always on the up and up. But none of those things ever affected our relationship; or so I thought.

The saying everybody wanted to be like the Joneses might not be true in all instances, but as I thought back over things, Jason's biggest problem was he wanted to be like me: Royce Jones.

Although, as long as I could remember my family had always had money; my father and grandfather taught me responsibility. I didn't get a free ride because I was a Jones. I had to work and earn my allowance.

I was never flashy, but I did like nice things and because I worked hard, I didn't see anything wrong for having them. I worked hard and played hard. But whatever I had, I always freely shared with Jason.

I wish I would've recognized that Jason had been envious of me before now. Maybe if I had, I wouldn't have invited him into my home; had him around my wife, and later around my kids.

I trusted him like a brother, but yet he betrayed me by sleeping with Lexi and then later with my eighteen-year-old daughter. No, I didn't kill Jason, but I was guilty of wanting to wrap my hands around his neck with the end result of me strangling the life out of him.

One of the guards came to my cell. "You have a visitor."

"I already had a visitor for today," I stated.

"It's your attorney," the guard said.

I left the jail cell and walked behind the prison guard. He opened up the door to a conference room where they allowed prisoners to speak one on one with their attorneys.

"Royce, how are you?" Mitch asked.

"Waiting to hear some good news from you," I responded, as I sat down across from him.

"I wish I had something good to tell you. The DA has sent another plea deal. For your confession, they are willing to give you twenty years."

"I'm fifty years old so that means I would be seventy when I get out. No. I won't sign that."

"But you know if we take this to court, you could get more time. It's possible you might get sentenced to death."

"I'm innocent. I did not kill anyone. Why aren't the police out there trying to find the real killer?"

The attorney stared me in the eyes. "Because in their eyes, you are the real killer."

I was trying my best not to feel defeated. I remained silent.

The attorney slipped a big brown envelope to me. "I'm going to leave you with some things they've discovered during their investigation. Read over them. Then tell me, how I can help you."

My attorney left me alone in the room staring at the brown envelope.

CHAPTER 3

Charity

"I just came back from seeing your daddy," Mom said as we sat across from each other at my kitchen table in the condo my parents used to finance. I could afford to take care of the bills myself, now that my event planning business had been bringing in income.

"How is he doing? I know I should go see him, but I can't bear to see him behind bars," I said.

"Charity, do you think I like seeing Royce like that? No, I don't, but I go see him so he knows that he's not going through this alone. He needs to see you. He wants to see you."

I'd written Dad but after seeing him a few times in handcuffs, it had left me emotionally depleted. I hadn't seen him face-to-face in over two weeks. I realized I was being selfish, but it was hard. It was difficult seeing him in that situation.

"Okay, I'll go," I finally broke down and said.

"Good. Well, you have to wait until next week now. We can go together."

"Fine."

"And Charity?"

"Ma'am," I responded.

"Don't flake out on me. In fact, I'll come pick you up to make sure you'll be there."

I stood and poured us each a glass of orange juice.

Mom looked at hers. "I was hoping for something a little stronger."

I retrieved a bottle of vodka from the cabinet and poured some in her glass.

She nursed it. "Now this is more like it."

I normally didn't drink around her, but as stressed out as I was, I needed a drink myself. I poured some vodka into my glass, stirred it with my juice and took a sip.

"What did Dad say about his case? Are they going to let him out now that they know he didn't kill Uncle Jason?"

"Dear, this is why I'm here. I'm going to need you and your sister's and brother's help. The police are convinced that Royce killed Jason."

"So what are you saying?"

"They aren't looking to find his real killer so it's up to us to find out who actually did it."

"Are you serious? They really think Dad did this. Oh, my goodness!" I felt myself having a panic attack.

"Charity, calm down." Mom reached across the table and placed her hand over mine.

I felt my breathing ease up some.

"Mom, Dad can't go to prison. What will we do?"

She laughed. I didn't see anything funny. She responded, "Dear, you are your mother's child. I thought I was dramatic, but baby girl, you got me beat."

"Mom, I'm not trying to be dramatic. This is serious. If we don't do something, he's going to be sent to Angola. We can't let this happen. He's innocent and the police are not doing their damn job."

"I'm going to let you slide with cursing around me, but watch your tone, young lady."

"Mom, tell me what I need to do. We need to call a family meeting. We've got to get Dad out of there."

"You're right. I want you to tell Hope to meet me at the house tonight around seven. I've already texted Lovie to meet us there around that time as well. What have I always stressed to you?"

"We're Joneses and together we'll get through anything," I replied.

"Exactly. So put your big-girl panties on. Put your thinking cap on and come tonight and be prepared to strategize."

Mom drank the rest of her drink. "I need another drink, but since I have to drive home, I'll wait until I get home before fixing me another."

"I'm worried about you. You're in that big house all by yourself. I noticed you're always drinking, but I rarely see you eat anything."

"I'm fine. You concentrate on taking care of yourself. I'm all right," she assured me.

She gave me a tight hug and kiss on the cheek and left.

I looked out the window and watched her pull off. I picked up the phone and made a call. "May I speak to Detective Omar Underwood," I asked the receptionist.

After a few clicks and some silence, I heard, "This is Detective Underwood; how may I help you?"

"This is Charity. What time do you get off?"

"Hi, baby. I'm headed out now. I can swing by there, if you need to talk."

"Please do. There's something I want to discuss with you, but not over the phone."

Less than an hour later, Omar and I were greeting each other with a hug and long sensuous kiss in the living room. Having his muscular arms wrapped around my small waist made me feel safe and secure. He'd recently gotten a promotion to detective so he no longer wore a police uniform but instead wore slacks, shirts and jackets.

"Baby, if you don't stop that, you're going to get me in trouble," Omar said. "I'm still on duty."

I licked my lips. "That's never stopped you before."

"You're right. It hasn't." He began to ravish my lips.

I pulled away. "Hold up. That's not why I called you here."

"You're such a tease," he joked.

I grabbed his hand and led him to the couch. "You're working homicide, aren't you?"

"Yes. But before you ask, I'm not working your father's case."

I curled up next to him. "But if I needed some information, you would be able to tell me, now, wouldn't you?"

"It depends. Some things are confidential and I wouldn't be able to share them with you."

I pulled back and looked at him. "So even if it's information that could possibly help free my father, you wouldn't share it with me?"

"No, I'm not saying that. Some things are only supposed to be accessed by the detectives working on the case. I'm not working on his situation so I might not have access to everything."

I sighed. I took his hand in my hand. "I've got a dilemma."

"Please don't ask," Omar said before I could finish.

"I need you. If you do this for me, I promise you I will never ask you for anything else."

Omar shook his head. "Charity. Don't." He placed his hands over his ears.

"Omar, I need you to get me the information in my father's files. I need to know what the police have on him so my family can work on proving that they're wrong."

I used my hands and removed his hands from over his ears. "Will you or won't you help me?" I batted my eyes.

Omar bit his bottom lip. "Charity."

"Pleassee." I pouted.

"Fine. Okay. I'm not supposed to, but for you. Only for you. But you have to promise me one thing."

"What? Anything," I responded.

"Do not share the information with anyone outside of your family. I mean it. It's for your eyes only."

"I promise you have nothing to worry about. When we finish it, we'll shred it."

"I can't believe you've got me risking my job like this. But for you, girl, I'll do anything," Omar said.

"And I appreciate it. I really do," I said, right before pushing him back on the couch and straddling him.

CHAPTER 4

Hope

It would've been nice to arrive home and not find Omar's car there. He'd practically moved in. If I said anything to Charity about it, she would've sworn I was "hating" on her. After the ordeal with Tyler, I couldn't have cared less about having a steady man.

Tyler was a thorn in my side. When I met him, I had no idea he was also dating my sister Charity. People always said that Charity and I could pass for twins with our cocoa brown complexion and high cheekbones, but we weren't twins. At twenty-two, I was two years younger than her and we wore our hair in different styles and colors. I dyed my hair from the original jet-black color to auburn.

I fell in lust with Tyler immediately. In the end, he'd had a secret vendetta against my father and had set out to destroy my, and Charity's, lives in the process. Charity saw through his charade, but I had fallen for him.

Tyler had me hoodwinked. When things escalated beyond Tyler's control, he'd held me hostage, confronted Dad with a gun and during a struggle for the gun, it had gone off resulting in Tyler's death. That tragic incident lingered in the back of my mind.

After all of that and also having to deal with everything going on with our dad, a relationship was the furthest thing on my mind. Right now I was simply trying to remain sane in the insanity going on around me.

"Charity," I called out. That was my signal to warn her that I was home.

I guess I was a little too late. I saw Charity topless on top of Omar on the couch.

"Hope, what are you doing here? I thought you would be gone for at least another hour."

I held up the shopping bags. "It didn't take as long as I thought. But I'm going to let you two finish doing what you were doing."

I had to laugh out loud because merely a year ago, Charity would've been on me about my sexual escapades, but at least I confined mine to the bedroom. I'd caught her screwing her man on our couch. I would never be able to look at that couch the same without thinking of it.

I went to the room we used for our home office and unpacked all of the office supplies I'd purchased.

To keep my mind off our troubles, I'd poured myself into Charity's event planning business. I'd purchased items so we could make the invitations for several of her clients' upcoming events.

I thought she was formatting the information so all we would have to do was print when I got back, but she had been preoccupied doing other things.

I was about to start typing when she burst through the door. I looked at her. "Is your company still here?"

"No, he's gone. Sorry you had to see that."

I shrugged my shoulders. "No biggie. You've seen me in some awkward positions."

"Don't remind me."

"Whatever," I said.

"I'm about to take a quick shower and then we can put the invitations together."

"You mean after I type and design them."

She walked in front of the computer. She moved the keyboard and did a few clicks. "Already done."

I looked on the computer screen and saw the designs. "Cool. I thought you hadn't."

"You should know it's business before pleasure for me. Now get those printed while I go shower."

By the time I was done halfway printing, Charity had returned. She was now wearing a pair of blue jeans and a pink t-shirt.

While stuffing envelopes, she said, "Mom stopped by earlier."

"How's she doing?" I asked.

"She pretends to be okay, but you know Mom."

"She's all about appearances," I added. I loved our mother, but sometimes she took being a Jones too far.

"She wants us to meet her at the house around seven. She wants to discuss how we're going to help free Dad."

"What do you mean? I thought he had a team of lawyers working on that."

"Hope, unfortunately, they are wanting him to plea bargain."

"For what? He didn't do anything. He's innocent."

"We know that, but they apparently feel like they have evidence to prove otherwise."

"Oh my God. If Dad goes to jail, what will happen to us?" I stopped stuffing envelopes.

"Hope, can you forget about yourself for one moment and think about what this is doing to Dad. Imagine what he's going through."

"I am thinking about Dad. He doesn't deserve to be locked up for something he didn't do."

"You're right and that's why tonight we're going to all come together and figure out a way to prove his innocence."

"How are we supposed to do that?" I asked.

"I don't know, but I'm sure Mom has it all figured out. I did ask Omar to help."

"He's part of the problem."

"Excuse me?" Charity got an attitude.

"Mr. Detective should be doing his job but he's not, and now Dad's in jail because of him."

"For your information, Omar has agreed to help me."

"How's that? He's going to give you the key to free Dad?" I asked.

"Possibly. He's going to get me the information in his file."

"I don't know how that's supposed to help."

I listened to Charity go on and on about her boyfriend Omar and what he was doing to help. I didn't like Omar. Never had and never would. I probably was a little biased because right now, all men were dogs except my dad and my brother, Lovie. Well, Lovie was a player, but he was my brother so he didn't get put in the same category as other men.

"Lighten up. Things are going to get better," Charity assured me.

I'm glad she had a positive attitude about our dad's situation, because I sure didn't. All I knew was that life as we knew it had changed forever the day the cops came to our house and arrested him.

I went to my room and pulled out some of the letters I'd received from him. I wiped the tears from my eyes as I read them. His words were meant to ease my mind about his situation, but they only reminded me of how selfish I'd been over the years. I'd taken so much for granted. I'd taken for granted that Dad would always be there for me, but now he wasn't.

He was behind bars and there weren't enough tears to get him out. I hoped Charity was right. I hoped the information Omar was supposed to give her would help us figure out a way to free Dad.

I didn't want to see him locked up for the rest of his life. I wanted Jason dead. I wished now that I hadn't wished it. If he were alive, we wouldn't have been going through this. Even in his death, Jason had wreaked havoc in all of our lives.

CHAPTER 5

Lovie

Mom's phone call about Dad left me feeling a little emotional. I felt it was my duty to make sure RJ Jones Funeral Home ran smoothly. I didn't want him to be concerned about the family business. He had enough on his mind; like his freedom.

I hated that in the past I'd given Dad a hard time about almost everything. I now realized he was only trying to leave a family legacy to me so I too could pass it down to my son. Fortunately, one of my uncles and Shannon, one of my cousins, were around to help make sure things ran smoothly in Dad's absence.

Shannon said over the intercom, "Slim's here."

Slim was the last person I wanted to see right at that moment. Before I could come up with an excuse not to see him, I was hearing a knock on the door. I was seated in Dad's office behind his desk.

"Come in," I spoke loudly.

The door opened and standing before me was Slim, who looked like the deceased rapper Big Pun's twin. He was minus his normal entourage of people. I stood and we shook hands.

"Have a seat," I said as I sat back down.

"Lovie, we miss you down at Bottom's Up," Slim said.

Bottom's Up was a popular club in the area. I used to be a regular, but with taking over the funeral homes, I didn't have much time to hang out. I had my father's business to run plus my own.

"Man, you know I've been busy. I'm still keeping the books straight, right? Any problems?" I asked.

"All is well. I wanted to check on you. How's your Pop doing?"

"He's hanging in there. I'm trying to maintain it out here so he'll have something to come back home to."

Slim looked around. "Looks like you got everything covered."

I knew Slim. We grew up together. He normally didn't come around unless he wanted something. I let him shoot the breeze for a minute before asking, "So what's up with you?"

"I came to offer my services."

I laughed. "I think you've been providing enough business."

Slim laughed. "Naw, man. People paying on time so I've cut down on the violence."

"What kind of services are you trying to offer?"

"My help, man. We both know your dad didn't kill your uncle Jason."

"You're right. He didn't. But how can you help me unless you know who did it?"

I had to tread lightly. Although Slim and I had grown up together, he was the last person you wanted to cross. His pockets ran deep and he was ruthless on the streets.

"Your dad's always been good to me. He knows what I do, but yet, he gave me respect. I want to help out any way I can."

"Thanks, Slim. I really appreciate the love. What's the word on the streets?"

"It's been quiet. Ain't heard nobody talking, but I can shake things up a little." Slim pulled out a roll of money. "Money talks."

"If you hear anything, let me know."

"I got your back." Slim stood up. "I got a few more stops to make, but you know the number if you need me."

Slim left out. Actually, I thought Slim was behind Jason's death. Maybe he was. Maybe he only showed up to see what I knew. Then again, Slim might have actually been sincere. He was really concerned and wanted to help me. So many questions went back and forth in my head.

Two hours later, I was sitting on the sofa at my parents' house. Mom appeared stressed. No amount of makeup could hide the stress lines all over her face. My two sisters looked okay under the circumstances. Charity kept texting someone. Probably Omar, her boyfriend, a man I still didn't like or trust. Hope pretended to be strong, but out of all of us, she was the most vulnerable.

Her ex-boyfriend Tyler did a number on her. If he wasn't already dead, I would've killed him. I had to pull myself together. I had to be strong. My family needed me.

"Mom, we're all here. We're ready to hear what you have to say," I said.

Charity placed her phone down. Hope looked in Mom's direction.

Mom stopped pacing back and forth and took a seat in what was normally my father's seat.

She looked each one of us in the eye before saying, "I've been trying to give the police the opportunity to clear up this situation, but after talking to Royce and our attorney, I realize I put faith in a system that's not working."

"The system's never been fair to the black man," I said.

"Lovie, that's true, but that's a conversation for another day. For now, I want to specifically concentrate on how we're going to help Royce."

Charity said, "I've asked Omar to help."

"You shouldn't have done that," I said.

"Why not? He's on the inside. He can find out stuff that we can't," she stated.

Mom said, "Charity. That's great. But we can't depend on out-siders to do what we will have to do ourselves."

"I agree," Hope said.

"What's your grand plan?" Charity asked Mom.

"We need to run our own investigation. We need to figure out who had reasons to kill Jason other than us."

"I could name a few people. A few people he's cheated," I declared.

"Then that's where we need to start. Find out where these people were around the time Jason was killed," she said.

"Mom, maybe we should hire a private investigator. Whoever killed Uncle...I mean, Jason is still out there. We don't know who did it and I don't want to worry about your safety," I said.

"I thought of that, but that's where I need your help. I need you to find someone."

"Consider it done," I said.

Charity said, "No need to. I already found us someone."

"Your boyfriend is not who I had in mind," I replied.

"But..." Charity said.

"Lovie, maybe Charity is right. We'll see what Omar has to say and see what happens."

I disagreed with Mom's decision. "Fine. Charity, call Omar. Tell him to get here ASAP."

CHAPTER 6

Omar

Before meeting Charity, I didn't believe in love at first sight. From the moment I saw her, I realized I had to make her mine. When the opportunity presented itself for me to introduce myself, I took it.

My feelings for her were the reason why I was now sitting there across the table from her family. Her mom, Lexi, could intimidate the strongest of men so I was doing my best not to be unnerved by her strength. She was a force not to be reckoned with.

"Omar, we do appreciate you coming here tonight."

"Mrs. Jones, as I was telling Charity earlier, I'm really not supposed to be looking at Mr. Jones' file. But I could not sit back and do nothing; especially after Charity asked me to."

Lovie said, "Spill it. What did you find out?"

I pulled my iPhone from my pocket and opened up a file. "There was a witness identifying Royce's car."

"Dad and Uncle Jason were friends. That's not unusual for them to visit one another," Lovie said as he leaned back in his chair.

I cleared my throat. "The witness also stated they saw Royce speeding away out of the driveway the night before Jason's body was discovered. The roaring of the engine is what got his attention and the reason why he looked out of his window in the first place."

"Which neighbor is this?" Lexi asked.

I debated on whether to divulge the information. "It's not relevant."

Lexi insisted, "It is. I may need to question this so-called witness."

"Mrs. Jones. Why don't you let me do the questioning?"

"Because, as you said, you're not supposed to be working on the case. If you start asking questions, I'm sure it'll get back to your boss, and then what?"

All eyes were on me as they waited on my response. Mrs. Jones did have a point, but her going around asking questions would be risky and could be dangerous.

"The neighbor was William Franklin. His house..."

"I know exactly where his house is. Right across from Jason's. That old man is blind in one eye and can't see out the other," Lexi interrupted me and said.

"Well, Mrs. Jones, according to the detective's notes, they also had other witnesses."

"Who?" she asked.

"The neighbor next door says they heard something the morning of the fire."

"But did they see Royce's car that morning?" Lexi asked.

"Mom, Omar's not the one who wrote the report," Charity stepped in and said.

"I didn't say he did. He's reading off things from the report. I want to know answers. Specifics."

"Charity, that's okay. It's a tense situation. To answer your question, Mrs. Jones, it doesn't mention that this neighbor saw a car. They only heard noises."

Lovie chimed in. "Nothing you've said thus far proves anything. I can see the cops questioning Dad, but to arrest him? None of it proves anything."

I go on and read more of the report. "The neighbor across the street."

"Mr. Franklin?" Hope asked, which was the first time I'd heard her say something tonight.

I looked up and responded, "Yes. He stated that Mr. Jones was visiting Jason earlier and he heard loud voices as if they were arguing. He also said he saw Mr. Jones leave and he was rubbing his fist when he exited the victim's house."

Lexi said, "So once again, the police are basing their findings on a man who is half-blind and probably deaf."

"Mom, we don't know that about Mr. Franklin," Charity said.

"You don't, but I do."

Lovie said, "What about a weapon? If our dad shot him, where's the smoking gun?"

I scanned the report. "There's no mention of locating a weapon. If they had found one, it would be in this report."

"No gun. Shaky witnesses. Why in the hell is my husband in jail?"

"Mrs. Jones, the DA thinks there's enough circumstantial evidence to show and prove that your husband had motive to kill him."

"But you haven't said anything in the report to convince me of that."

"The victim's secretary said he and you were having an affair. That Mr. Jones found out about it and came to confront him about it in the office one day. That things got heated and Mr. Jones stormed out. She also mentioned that you and he also got into a heated discussion."

"That trick doesn't know what she's talking about. I will contact her and deal with her myself." Lexi sounded highly upset. "If you're going to eavesdrop, make sure you get the full story before going back telling half-truths. Yes, I confronted Jason about some things, and yes, he pissed me off, but she wasn't in the room so she has no idea what he and I were arguing about."

Lovie went and stood by Lexi. "Mom, you've got to calm down.

I'm afraid you'll have a stroke or something. We can see the veins on your forehead."

"Hope, pour me a drink," Lexi commanded.

Hope got up to follow her orders.

Charity said, "Mom, don't you think you've drunk enough for one day?"

Lexi gave Charity a look that scared me. "I don't need you or anyone else to monitor me. Hope, drink, please."

Hope hurried and left the room.

Lexi turned toward me. "Omar, I need you to get me Jason's secretary's address. I need to make a house call."

"Mrs. Jones, I don't think that's a good idea. You're upset and she can claim you're harassing her. Besides, you're not supposed to know she talked to the police. I can't have people checking to see who accessed the records. If they do, my name will be written all over it. I can't lose my job. Besides, if I lose my job, I won't be able to assist you."

"Fine. I'll table it for now. But eventually, someone will need to talk to her."

Hope returned with the drink. Lexi took the glass and drank it all with one big gulp.

Charity looked at me. I looked at her. "Maybe I should wait to discuss everything else at a later time."

"Too much time has already passed by. We need to know every-thing and now," Lexi stated.

I spent the next thirty minutes going over what was in the file. Afterward, Charity walked me to the door.

"Thanks for everything, Omar. I'll call you when I get home."

"Why don't you stop by my place? I hate to see you like this. Let me put a smile on your face." I kissed her on the cheek and left.

CHAPTER 7

Lexi

I took a few deep breaths before exiting the car. I glanced at the remnants of what was left of Jason's house. It was surprising to me Jason's body could be identified after seeing the damage the fire had done.

I walked across the street to Jason's neighbor's house. Before I could knock on the door, the door swung open. An elderly man about seventy years old greeted me. "Lexi, dear, what are you doing here?"

I walked up to Mr. Franklin and hugged him. "I came to check on you, of course."

He blushed. "Come on in."

He wobbled a little while walking with a cane. I followed him to his living room.

"Help yourself to something to drink. I've got some juice and water in the frigerator," Mr. Franklin said.

"Mr. Franklin, I'm fine." I walked to the window facing Jason's house. I eased the curtain back. "Mr. Franklin, the kids and I have been debating about something. Maybe you can clear it up. What color do you think my car is?"

"Well, Lexi, I don't know."

"Look. It's right outside." I pointed. I moved out of the way so he could look out the window at my car that was parked in what used to be Jason's driveway.

"It looks blue to me."

"You sure it doesn't look black to you?" I asked.

"No, ma'am. I might be old, but I know my colors."

"Calm down, Mr. Franklin," I said as I gently touched him on the arm.

We went and sat down on his sofa.

"How's Royce?" he asked.

"As well as can be expected under the circumstances."

"I really hated to hear about him getting arrested. You know I think he's innocent," Mr. Franklin said.

"But if you thought he was innocent, why did you lie and tell the police you saw Royce's car at Jason's the night before?" I blurted out without thinking.

"They must have misunderstood," he stuttered. "I said a car looking like Royce's. I never said it was Royce's car."

"The car that's outside now is Royce's car. Did you realize that?"

He dropped his head. "I...I didn't. I assumed it was yours." His hand started shaking.

"What else did you see that night?"

"I told the police everything," he responded.

"My husband's freedom is at stake and I need for you to tell me what you told them," I said in a soft voice, although inside I was far from being calm. In the inside, I wanted to slap him until he revealed what he had seen to me.

"I heard an engine roar up and I rushed to my window and that's when I saw a car speed away. It looked like Royce's car. He had stopped by earlier."

"About that. What was Royce doing there earlier?" I asked, as if I didn't already know.

"I don't know. I heard loud voices. It made me rush to my window. I saw Royce come out rubbing his hand. He jumped in his car and drove off."

"When did you notice the fire?"

"I get up early. I thought I smelled smoked. I checked my house and didn't find anything. I stepped out on the porch and that's when I saw the smoke coming from Jason's house."

"What did you do next?" I asked.

"I called nine-one-one. I started yelling, 'Fire! Fire!' and other people came out of their houses."

"During the night, did you see anything else? Hear anything else?"

"Lexi, I think it's time that you leave."

I remained seated. "No. Not until you tell me what else you saw that night."

Mr. Franklin glared at me. "What makes you think I saw anything else?"

"Because if you hadn't, you would have said you didn't." I stood up. "I'm going to leave for now, but know this. I will be back. And when I come back, be prepared to tell me what else you saw."

He clutched his heart as if he was in distress. "I need my pills." He reached for them in his pocket.

He was taking too long for me. Last thing I wanted was for him to have a heart attack on me. I went into of his pocket and located the pillbox. I popped one in his mouth.

He started breathing more evenly. "Thank you. Thank you."

"I'm glad you're all right."

"Every now and then my heart beats a little too fast."

"I understand," I replied. "Look, Mr. Franklin, I'm not trying to upset you. I'm only trying to bring my husband home."

He nodded. "If I remember anything else, I'll call you."

I hugged him. "I'll be back to check on you."

The moment I stepped out of his house, I heard him slam and lock the door.

I kept walking toward my car but detoured to the next-door

neighbor's house. I rang the doorbell and knocked, but no one came to the door. I noticed Mr. Franklin peeping out his window. When he saw me looking in his direction, he closed the curtain.

Something was telling me he knew more than he'd told me, or the police. If he did, I would find out about it. I wasn't going to pressure him about it right then, but I would be back.

I contemplated on whether to walk around Jason's house. My thoughts were interrupted by an urgent text from Charity. I hopped in my car and sped over to her place.

She greeted me at the door looking as if she'd lost her best friend. Tears were flowing down her face.

I took her in my arms. "What's wrong, baby?"

"I now know why they really think Dad killed Uncle Jason."

I pulled away. "What's going on, Charity?"

"Follow me," she said.

I followed her and there sitting in the living room were also Lovie and Hope.

Charity said, "Mom, have a seat."

Once again, I did as instructed. All three sets of eyes were looking at me. I looked at the sad expression on each one of their faces.

CHAPTER 8

Royce

I spent the next few days after Mitch's visit reading over the files he had given me. I didn't know how I was going to tell Lexi about what I'd discovered. The information showed I'd had every reason for wanting Jason dead. The police evidence disclosed documents proving Jason had been stealing money from me for years. In one of the officers' notes, there was mention of Jason and Lexi's affair, leading to concerns regarding Lovie's paternity. Jason's secretary claimed I threatened to kill Jason because of all of the drama.

I couldn't deny that I didn't think about killing him. I couldn't even deny that I'd had intentions of killing him, but regrettably, someone else had already beaten me to it. The only crime I'd committed was not reporting it.

The information gave the police just cause to believe I was responsible for the murder. The information in the file, however, didn't provide proof of my DNA. According to the notes, the body was so burnt that Forensics was unable to extract any. The police were also unsuccessful in locating the weapon used to shoot and kill Jason prior to the fire.

If the police knew of Jason's unscrupulous business practices, then I shouldn't have been their only suspect. It frustrated me to realize that while I was locked up, the real killer was roaming around free. Jason had done enough damage to my family. I hadn't revealed to Mitch I'd discovered Jason's dead body the night before. I didn't want to give the police any reason to arrest Lexi or Lovie.

I needed to prove their theories wrong. One of them could be squashed immediately. I exited my cell and went toward the phones located in the center of the dormitory. There were four phones that 150 men had to share. To make matters worse, only three were operational. That day, it seemed like everyone else had the same idea and wanted to make calls to their loved ones as well.

I spoke to some of the men whom I'd known when we were all out on the streets. I'd buried some of their family members or had attended church with some of their mothers. I waited impatiently in line to use the pay phone.

"Pops, you can use it now," a young man said.

Some of the other men grumbled, but I didn't care. I walked ahead of them and dialed Lovie's number. I called a couple of times but didn't get an answer. I then dialed Mitch's number.

The recording said, "We have a collect call from Royce Jones, an inmate in the Caddo Correctional Center. Press one to accept this call or press five to block this call."

I heard a few clicks and then Mitch's voice. "Royce, how are you?"

"Mitch, I need you to get in contact with Lovie. I need for you to set up a DNA test so we can prove to the courts that he is my child." If truth be told, I also wanted to erase the tiniest of doubts that had been in the back of my mind since discovering Jason and Lexi had slept with each other behind my back. In my heart, I felt like Lovie was my son, but the DNA would prove it.

"I will. I take it you've read the files."

"Yes, and if we can at least prove that one thing, maybe we can go about disproving some of those other accusations."

"Since these phone calls are recorded, I'm going to stop you from saying anything else," Mitch said. "We can discuss further strategy during my next visit. In the meantime, I will contact Lovie and get the DNA test scheduled. I will have a specialist stop by and collect a swab sample from you, but I need to obtain an approval from the courts prior to that. As soon as I can, we'll get that rolling. In the meantime, keep studying the information. If you can find any other loopholes, let me know. But not on this phone."

"You have one minute left on this call," the computer-operated voice informed us.

"Fifteen minutes go by fast," I blurted out.

"Yes, they do. Royce. Stay prayerful," Mitch said.

"I'm trying," I said right as the phone disconnected.

The line behind me had gotten longer. I wanted to hear Lexi's voice but decided to go back to my cell and write her a letter instead. In the letter, I shared with her some of the things I'd discovered. I asked her to stay strong for the kids. I mentioned she didn't have to worry about me. I tried to reassure her Mitch and the rest of the attorneys would get me out of this mess. I thought if I kept telling her that, I would eventually believe it myself.

I also tried to include a memory of when we'd first met. The day I realized I had fallen in love with her. The day she'd admitted to sharing those same feelings. I wanted to hold on to the memories of yesterday because only God knew when I would be able to be with my family again.

"Chow time," one of the trustees said, right before handing me a tray of food. Instead of the inmates going to a cafeteria, trays of food were brought to us by trustees. Trustees were prisoners who were given their position due to good behavior or the nature of their crime.

The piece of meat was a mystery and the potatoes looked soft, but when you put the fork in them, they were hard as a brick. The only edible thing on the plate was the roll. I removed a can of Vienna sausages from under my bunk and used the roll to make me a sandwich.

I had to laugh out loud at the irony. I had a million dollars in the bank, but yet here I was behind bars, and for dinner I was eating a Vienna sausage sandwich. Money could buy a lot of things, but was it enough to buy my freedom?

CHAPTER 9

Charity

Now that Mom and my two siblings were seated in the living room, I shared with them some of the other things Omar divulged to me. When Omar first approached with the information, I didn't want to believe him. But the proof was right there in black and white. I had so many questions that only Mom could answer them.

"Mom, I'm sorry I got a little emotional earlier. I'm calm now."

"You've got me worried," she stated.

I looked at Hope and at Lovie. "We were talking before you got here. We mean no disrespect when we ask you this, because your answer may help Dad."

"Child, what is it? Spit it out."

"Is Lovie Dad's son or Jason's?" Lovie could have gotten his Hershey chocolate complexion from either one. I felt compelled to ask.

Mom's face went blank. She took in a few deep breaths. "I don't know where this is coming from. But we will not be having this discussion," she responded.

I picked up a piece of paper on the table and handed it to her. She looked at it and read it. She looked up at me. "I can explain."

"Explain the fact that your indiscretion with Uncle Jason may be the reason why Dad's locked up," Hope blurted out.

Mom stood. "Young lady, you will not take that tone with me. I don't owe you kids an explanation, but since you want to be in grown folks' business, I will share some things with you."

I took a seat next to Lovie. Lovie remained quiet throughout the entire ordeal. For some reason he was calm. If it had been me, I would've been totally upset.

"Your uncle Jason took advantage of me during a weak time in my life. Yes, we slept together, once."

Hope gasped. "How could you do this to Dad?"

"Hope, let her talk," I said.

She went on to say, "During that time, Royce was spending an incredible amount of time away from home. Every weekend he was going over to Marshall, Texas to be with his other woman; Tyler's mom. I felt abandoned. Jason kept feeding me information and one night, in a drunken state of mind, I succumbed to him. I've regretted that one-time incident ever since." Tears flowed down her face.

Lovie got off the couch and wrapped his arm around her shoulder. "Mom, it's okay. Uncle Jason was a rat. He hurt you. He hurt Dad and all of us. I don't want you to keep holding on to that guilt."

Hope said, "But what about Lovie? You never answered Charity's question."

"I don't know. I just don't know. In my heart, he's Royce's, but to be honest, I just don't know." She started crying and her body shook. Lovie had to hold Mom up. We'd seen her cry before but never liked this.

Lovie glared at me. "Are you satisfied now? I told you this wasn't a good idea."

Mom waved her hand. "That's okay, Lovie. It needed to be discussed." She faced Lovie. "I keep feeling your phone vibrate. Answer it. It might be important."

Lovie looked at her. "There's nothing more important than my family."

I said, "It may be Dad."

"I hadn't thought of that." Lovie looked at his phone. "Dad's tried to call me several times. That's the number from the jail." He held out his cell phone so we could see the number. "Mitch called me too," he added.

"Call him back and see what he wants," Mom insisted.

Lovie called him and placed the call on speaker. "Mitch, this is Lovie. I'm with the family and I have you on speaker."

"Good. I talked to Royce."

Mom asked, "Is he okay?"

"Lexi, yes, he's fine. He sends his love."

Lovie asked, "Then what's going on?"

Mitch responded, "I'm not sure of what you all know. But Royce has asked me to set up a DNA test to prove to the courts that you are his son and not Jason's."

"But what if..." my voice trailed off.

"He's Royce's son and this will settle it for once and for all," Mom said.

"Good. I'm glad you're confident, Lexi. This will help the defense if it does come back proving Royce is Lovie's father."

"When do I need to come take the test?" Lovie asked.

"That's the thing. I'm required to get a court order first. Once I do, I'll be in touch. It shouldn't take more than a day or two."

"Thanks, Mitch," Mom said.

Lovie hung up the phone.

Mom said, "See, after this test, we can put all of this behind us."

I was still upset that Mom had been so careless and because of that, Lovie and I might not have shared the same biological father. It's funny how you always think your parents are just parents. Rarely do you see them as people who are going through life's struggles exactly like you. Mom was my mother. Up until lately, I hadn't really looked at her as a woman with pain or desires like I would have.

Mom sighed. "I realize it may be hard, but please don't let this affect our relationship. I love each and every one of you. I would give my life for you all."

"It won't, Mom," I assured her as I gave her a tight hug.

Hope remained quiet. She sat with her lips poked out.

Mom took a seat next to Hope. "Can y'all leave us alone? Hope and I need to have a little talk."

I motioned for Lovie to follow me. We were now in the kitchen. I gave him a can of Coke from the refrigerator. I poured myself a glass of water. We stood by the kitchen counter in silence.

"Are you scared about the DNA?" I asked.

"Nope. Regardless of what the DNA says, Royce Jones is my father."

I agreed. I gave him a tight hug. I didn't want to think about the aftermath if the DNA results showed differently.

CHAPTER 10

Hope

Charity and Lovie were in another room. I really didn't want them to leave me alone with Mom. She didn't like it when any of us got sassy with her. But I was disappointed in her. How could she not know who Lovie's daddy was? I expected more from her. She'd always been my role model.

"Hope, I'm talking to you and expect for you to respond."

I rolled my eyes. "I don't feel like talking."

"I'm going to ignore the eye rolling because it's a stressful situation. But I suggest you get control of it before I forget and go old school on you. Understood?"

I still didn't say anything.

"Understood!" she repeated.

"Yes, ma'am," I responded.

"Good. Now, baby girl, I understand why you're upset. I'm upset as well. I should've said something to Royce years ago and if I had, maybe he wouldn't have done what he did to you."

I didn't want Mom feeling guilty about me sleeping with Jason. I was eighteen. I understood what I was doing. It wasn't her fault I'd always had a secret crush on Jason.

I spoke out. "It's not your fault Uncle Jason took advantage of my naïveté."

"If he wasn't part of our lives, then maybe none of this would have happened." Mom stood and walked to the mantel. She picked up the picture frames filled with pictures of the family.

She turned and faced me. "You and I are more alike than you know. You have that free spirit and fire in you like I did at your age. Don't let what Jason or Tyler did to you kill that."

"Mom, I don't want to talk about either one of them."

"You need to because if you run away from it, you'll never be able to move past things. Don't do like I did and pretend like it never happened."

She sat back down beside me. The anger I had felt about her actions slowly disappeared.

"Mom, I'm sorry about earlier."

"No apology needed."

"Can you answer one last question, please?" I asked.

"What?"

"Did Jason rape you?"

She placed her hand on top of mine. "No, dear. Although he took advantage of me by getting me drunk and enticing me, I was unfortunately a willing participant in what we did. Yes, I felt violated but it wasn't rape."

"That's how I feel sometimes. I feel like he violated me. I feel like he took away my innocence." For the first time I'd said what I'd been feeling for years. The tears I'd been suppressing finally fell. It was like a floodgate had opened; I couldn't stop.

Mom wrapped her arm around me and held me. "Let it out." She patted me on the back as I closed my eyes and let her rock me back and forth with her.

She continued to say, "Jason's gone and he will not be able to hurt you or any of us ever again."

I continued crying. Mom handed me some tissue from off the table. In between sniffles, I managed to say, "I come across as a spoiled brat sometimes, but there's more to me than what people realize."

"I know there is, dear."

"When we were going through our money issues, I found out who my real friends were. And truthfully, Charity's the only one I could depend on. When I stopped splurging and spending money on my friends, they stopped returning my calls."

"Then they weren't your real friends to start off with," she disclosed. "I didn't like the people you were hanging around with anyway. They looked like opportunists. What about Maria? You two used to be close at one time."

"We were close until her boyfriend tried to talk to me. I told Maria about it and she accused me of going after him. Which was a total lie, Mom, because I would never do anything like that to Maria."

"Love will make women turn on their friends. The last time I saw Maria's mom, she mentioned Maria was depressed over some loser."

"That's probably him."

"Maybe you can use this time to go make things right with her."

I wasn't so sure I wanted to do that. Maria's lack of trust in me really damaged our friendship. "She said some hateful things to me, too. She accused me of being a self-centered, spoiled brat."

Mom laughed. I didn't see anything funny. She rubbed my hand. "You have to admit you do like to have your way."

"But there's nothing wrong with that," I said.

"No, there isn't. But when you don't get your way, you do like to pout."

"But..." Then I stopped talking. She was right. In fact Maria was right to some extent, but she was my friend. She didn't have to say all of those things to me. I did need to make some changes.

Mom brushed my hair out of my face. "Look at you. You're beautiful. You're smart. You have your father's sense of humor. You have my street smarts. Baby girl, you are a diamond. Know your worth. Never ever again allow any man to make you feel less than the precious jewel that you are."

"Mom, confidence has never been an issue for me."

"On the surface, it appears that way, but underneath." She touched my chest. "You were insecure. You know why I know? I was like you at one point. I pretended to be Ms. Confidence so that my insecurities wouldn't show. "

She was right. I tried to overcompensate for things because of some of my insecurities. "I'm going to work on being a better me," I said.

"You have good qualities, dear. Work on loving yourself more. And try to show a little more compassion for others. Everyone is not out to get you," she said.

"I know. But they sure are out to be like me."

"Well, I can't disagree with you on that. Because..."

We said in unison, "Everybody wants to be like the Joneses."

We laughed together. I felt better about everything. I even felt hopeful about Dad's situation. I hoped and prayed when the DNA tests were done, it proved he was Lovie's father and not Jason.

CHAPTER 11

Lovie

I'd seen some interesting things happen while sitting in the waiting room of the hospital. I'd overheard a conversation between a couple that was having marital problems due to the woman's infidelity. I witnessed a couple's grief after losing their only child. I witnessed the miracle of a woman being saved after having a heart attack. I surfed the Internet on my phone and posted a few things on my Facebook page.

I kept watching the door, hoping that my name would be the next one called. Mitch was able to get me in to do a test within a couple of days like he had promised. I only wished it had been at another location; someplace that didn't take forever to call their patients back to be seen.

"Mr. Jones, we're ready for you," the petite nurse said from the doorway.

"Finally," I mumbled under my breath.

I followed the cute nurse back to an open door. "Have a seat and the tech will be here shortly."

I didn't know if I was supposed to take a seat on the bed or on the chair. I sat in the chair.

The lab technician knocked on the door and then walked in. "Mr. Jones," she said.

"Yes. That's me," I confirmed.

"I'm here to swab you and then you'll be on your way."

"Hold up. You don't have to take any blood or anything?" I asked.

"No, sir." She tore off the paper to what looked like a huge Q-tip. "Now open wide."

I did as instructed. She stuck the swab inside of my mouth and then placed it in a plastic envelope and sealed it. She wrote something on it and placed it in a container.

"That's it?" I asked.

"That's it. We should have the results back in a couple of days."

"Wow, that was not painful at all."

"It's one of the simplest tests that we do," she assured me.

"Thank you," I said.

I drove to the Caddo Correctional Center in silence. Now that the test was done, I would soon know something that had been weighing heavily on my mind since Mom had revealed what happened with Uncle Jason.

An hour later, I was seated across from Dad, looking at him through a glass partition and talking to him with the phone up to my ear.

"Son, I want you to know that regardless of what the DNA results say, you are my son. You hear me," he said.

I looked him in the eyes and nodded. "I know." I hoped I sounded convincing.

"How's your mom really doing?"

"She's handling it the best she can."

"And your sisters?"

I looked downward. "They were a little upset when they heard about the paternity test."

"How did they find out?"

I couldn't reveal to him that Omar had shared the information with Charity. Especially since I knew one of the guards was listening in on our conversation. We were the only ones in the visitation area so it was easy to overhear us.

"Let's simply say that Charity was the one who found out. So you know if she knew, she was going to tell Hope."

"I really hate they had to be put into the middle of all of this."

"Me too. But the tests are done. All we have to do now is wait."

Dad's eyes changed from brown to black. "I hate the day Jason became my friend."

"He had us all fooled," I said in my attempt to make him feel better.

"Your grandfather used to tell me Jason was jealous of me, but I wouldn't listen to him. I bet you he's rolling over in his grave, saying, 'I told you so.'"

"Dad, you can't keep beating yourself up over it. What we're trying to do is find evidence to show you couldn't have killed him." I wasn't supposed to tell him. I sure wasn't supposed to say it over a monitored phone. I simply wanted to say something to him to give him some hope.

"Son, what do you mean?"

"We're going to get you out of this, Dad."

"Lovie, I only want you to do two things: take care of your mother and sisters and the family business."

"I wish I could promise you that, but I can't. You've always taught me to be a man of my word. So Dad, as sure as my name is Lovie Jones, I will do whatever it takes to prove your innocence."

"Son, I'm giving you a direct order. Stay out of this and let the police do their job."

"And I'm telling you I'm not going to sit back and let them make up false evidence. The jurors will believe everything they show them so we have to make sure we're able to prove everything they have is incorrect and based on false pretenses. I will not be moved."

"I don't want to be up in here worried about your safety or your freedom. It doesn't make sense for both of us to be incarcerated."

I looked at him straight in the eyes. "Nothing is going to happen to me. But the real killer will not get away with what he's done. I'm not trying to find the real killer because I care about Uncle Jason. I'm trying to find the real killer to obtain your freedom. Right now, you're here because of a crime you didn't commit. The justice system is not fair."

"No, son, it's not always fair. But sometimes it is. I still don't think a jury would convict me."

"I can't trust that," I said.

"I love you for wanting to help me. But Lexi would kill me if she knew I put you in harm's way."

Little did Dad know that Mom was behind us searching for the real killer. I kept that information to myself since he seemed to be under enough stress.

"Dad, don't worry about a thing. I've got everything handled out here."

"Time's up," the guard said.

We said our goodbyes. A tear rolled from my left eye as I walked out.

CHAPTER 12

Omar

I stood in the doorway and watched Charity sleep. The more time I spent with her, the more I cared about her. I would do whatever I could to protect her. It'd been a few years since I'd found myself in a serious relationship. Some women were all about themselves, but not Charity.

As a police officer I'd seen a lot. She was like a light in an extremely dim, sick world. I hadn't always made the best decisions in life, and I hoped those bad ones didn't come back to bite me. Being around Charity made me want to be a better man.

My phone rang. Charity yawned. I walked inside of the room and got my phone from the nightstand. It was my partner.

"I'll be right there," I said after a brief conversation.

Charity said, "Who was that?"

"Baby, I got to go in."

Charity looked at the clock. "It's three o'clock in the morning."

"There was a robbery at the Franklin store."

Charity turned toward me. "Be careful."

"Always," I said, while looking for my belt.

Charity reached on the other side of the bed and handed me the belt I'd been looking for. "Here you go."

I bent and gave her a quick peck on the lips. "Thanks, babe."

"Let me get my stuff together so I can leave, too."

"You're welcome to stay here. Not sure of how long I'll be, but you're welcome to stay."

"You sure? Men tend to feel some kind of way about having a woman in their personal space when they're not around." She smiled.

"This man here doesn't have anything to hide. So baby, you're welcome to stay whether I'm here or not."

"Good. I'm still a little sleepy. You wore a sista out." She licked her lips.

"Don't do that with your lips. Got me having a woody and I've got to work this case."

"Get out of here," Charity said.

"I'm gone." I kissed her one more time and headed out.

❧

I pulled up in front of the Franklin store. There were several other police cars out front. The store had been secured with yellow tape and barriers. I noticed a couple of news vans up front as well.

"Detective, it's about time you showed up," said Sergeant Mills.

I ignored his negative tone. He was still upset I'd made detective. "Where's Jake?"

"You'll find your partner roaming around somewhere inside," he responded.

I took a survey of the area as I made my way inside. Jake, or Detective Ford, was picking up something and putting it in an evidence bag.

"So what do we have here?" I asked.

"Must have caught you in the middle of something?" Jake asked.

"You could say that. What's going on here?"

I followed behind him as he talked. "Strange thing. The person who broke in didn't take anything, but they sure destroyed a lot of the merchandise. They also left this note." He handed me a plastic bag with a typed note inside.

It read: *This is a warning. Next time, it might be you.*

"Where's the owner?" I asked.

"He should be here any minute. I sent a car to get him." He glanced outside. "In fact, there he is now."

"My store," Mr. Franklin said repeatedly as we walked out to meet him at the curb.

"Sir, I'm Detective Ford and this is my partner, Detective Underwood. We need to ask you a few questions."

I handed him the plastic bag that held the letter. "Do you know what this means?"

"I don't have my glasses on. I can't read this."

Jake said, "That's okay. I'll read it to you." He did as he said.

I noticed Mr. Franklin's hands shake. "I don't know why they're targeting me." His voice stuttered. "I've worked hard to maintain this store. I'm good to everyone in the neighborhood. I don't hurt anybody. Who would do something like this? This is going to cost thousands of dollars to fix."

"You have insurance, don't you?" I asked.

"I...I can get the insurance to pay to fix the front of the store, but the merchandise. It's been destroyed."

Someone else walked in, keeping up a lot of noise. "Uncle William, why didn't you call me? I had to hear about this from a news alert."

"This is my nephew, Sam."

"Sam, I'm Detective Underwood and that's Detective Ford. We were trying to find out from your uncle if he knew why someone would vandalize the store and leave a note."

I allowed him to see it. Sam read it and shook his head. "I have no idea. I've been managing the store since he's gotten up in age."

"Hold up, son. I can still take care of things if I wanted to," Mr. Franklin said.

"Yes, Uncle William, you could. I didn't mean anything by that."

"I'm just saying. Don't think 'cause I let you manage the store that I couldn't."

I listened to them go back and forth for a few minutes. Jake cleared his throat. He reached into his pocket. "Sam, here's our card. If you can think of anything or anyone, please let us know." He handed the card to Sam.

I reached in my pocket and did the same thing.

"Mr. Franklin," I said. "It's going to be all right. We will find out who did this to your store."

The forensics guys did their jobs. A few hours later, I was back at home. I opened up the door and soft music was playing. Charity stood in the kitchen cooking.

"Hey, baby, you're back."

She walked over to me and gave me a kiss.

I looked at the big breakfast she'd cooked. "Baby, you didn't have to cook me anything."

"I know I didn't have to. I wanted to. You've done so much for my family and me. This is the least I could do."

"Let me go freshen up some and I'll be right back," I said, while patting her on the butt.

"I'll be waiting." Her words purred off her lips.

I smiled. I was one lucky man to be coming home to a woman like Charity. I had to figure out a way to make it permanent.

CHAPTER 13

Lexi

It'd been a few days but still no word on the DNA test. It was the weekend so I really didn't expect to get any results until next week. I sat next to Charity in the visiting booth and watched her and her dad talk.

I never thought in a million years I would be visiting my man behind prison walls. One of the things I admired about Royce when I met him was that he wasn't like some of the other guys in my neighborhood. He always tried to do things by the book. But unfortunately, his friend Jason didn't.

Even in his death, Jason was wreaking havoc on our lives. Contrary to popular belief, everyone in Louisiana didn't practice or believe in voodoo, but if I did, I would have had Jason's spirit conjured up so I could try to kill him again.

Charity handed me the black phone. "Dad wants to talk to you."

I plastered on a fake smile. "Baby, you're looking a little better."

"Vienna sausages and sardines."

"Ugh. I can't see how you eat sardines," I blurted out and felt bad as soon as the words came out of my mouth. "I'm just glad you're eating. You had me worried."

"Did you get my last letter?" he asked.

"Yes."

"And are you doing what I asked you to do?" he asked.

I looked away. "Sort of."

"Lexi, *sort of* is not a yes."

"Fine, Royce. No. I'm not going to do it."

"Lexi, dear, I need you to get it done. If anything happens to me, I want you to have full power of attorney. I don't want you to run into any legal issues with my siblings."

"But nothing is going to happen to you. We're going to get you out of there."

"I'm trying to think positive, but I'm also trying to be realistic," Royce stated.

A guard walked in. I heard him say, "Two minutes."

"Baby, I've got to go. Please do it. Do it for me. Ease my mind. I only want to make sure you're legally protected."

"I will do it first thing Monday morning."

"Promise?" he asked.

I looked him in the eyes. "I promise."

"Now, let me see both of my girls smile."

"Charity, smile for your dad."

Charity did like I did, put on a fake smile.

"I love you both," he said.

"I love you too, baby," I reassured him.

I gave Charity the phone. "I love you," she said.

Royce hung up the phone on his end and we hung it up on our end.

Neither Charity nor I said anything as we walked back down the long hallway and to the car.

I dropped Charity off at home and then headed to RJ Jones Funeral Home.

The parking lot was filled to capacity when I arrived. I ended up parking about a block away due to the lack of available space.

One of the workers greeted me at the door. "Mrs. Lexi, we weren't expecting you here today."

"I wanted to stop by and check on things."

He closed the door. "We have one service going on in the chapel. We have people out at two other memorial services now. One at Galilee and the other at Corinth."

"Okay. Where's Lovie?" I asked.

"He's in his office, I think," the worker responded.

I peeked inside of the chapel. Everything had been set up nicely for the family. I eased down the hall to Royce's office. I knocked on the door. Lovie opened it.

"Mom, what are you doing here?"

I gave him a hug. "Everyone acts like I can't be here."

I walked inside and took a seat on the leather couch in the corner of the office.

"No, that's not it. You haven't been here in a while, that's all."

"I just came from seeing your dad."

"How is he?" Lovie asked.

"He's fine. He wants me to get some things switched over to my name. He feels if something else happens to him, his family might trip. He wants to secure our future."

"He's right. Some don't like the fact that I'm running things. But in reality, hardly anything has changed. Everyone's positions are still in place. Dad mainly dealt with scheduling and he left most of the other tasks to some of the other family members. He did do embalming and as you know I don't do that. Although I am in there when some procedures are done."

"Dear, you're doing a good job. I'm going to call Mitch on Monday so he can get those things set up. Of course, when your dad comes home, everything will reverse and it'll be back to status quo."

"Of course," Lovie said as he sat behind the desk.

"What I really came over here for was to check on you," I admitted.

"I'm fine. We're just waiting."

"Regardless of what those results say, Royce is your daddy."

"Mom, I'm not stressing over that," he voiced. He picked up a copy of *The Times* and handed it to me.

I read the headline. "Looks like I need to pay Mr. Franklin another visit."

"Mom, I think it's best that you don't. They may think we're behind it."

"Why would we want to vandalize his store?"

"They don't know what we do. They may think we're trying to scare him from testifying against Dad."

"Lovie, trust me. Mr. Franklin is no threat when it comes to that. Mitch will eat him alive on the witness stand."

"Slim wants to help out," Lovie said.

"Are you sure Slim's not the one who had Jason killed?"

"I don't think he did, but I wouldn't put it past him."

"Use your best judgment when dealing with Slim. He's friendly but ruthless."

Lovie agreed.

I stood. "Well, dear. Looks like you've got everything here under control. I've got a few more stops I want to make before heading home."

We hugged. I closed the door and sighed. I had to lean on the wall for a moment to catch my composure. Seeing Lovie behind Royce's desk instead of him did something to me.

CHAPTER 14

Royce

One thing about being in jail, you have nothing but time on your hands; too much time, in fact, to think. I'd replayed my whole life in my head over and over from my first memory until now. I remembered things I thought I had forgotten. Some of those memories were pleasant ones, but being there, it was hard to smile about them. Sometimes my mind would linger too long on the unpleasant memories causing me to feel pain. Pain that I thought I was over and was buried deep within my soul.

I tried to figure out what I could have done differently that would have resulted in another outcome. One of the things I will always regret is having an affair.

Instead of talking to Lexi about the problems we were having, I'd set out and had an affair with another woman. The other woman was no better than Lexi, but she'd made me forget my responsibilities. With her, I could be carefree. I grew to care for the woman, but I didn't love her like I loved Lexi. I got caught up in the affair and didn't know how to get out of it. Once I did decide to leave, it was too late.

I'd done damage to my relationship and put my wife in a position to be used by the likes of Jason. Jason had always been known as a ladies' man. He'd fathered kids he probably never claimed. He'd been guilty of sleeping with other men's wives, but I never thought he would stoop so low to do it to me. Hindsight is twenty-twenty. If I weren't so busy trying to sneak and cheat behind Lexi's back,

I would have seen the signs. I would have noticed the moment Jason's attention went from being a friend to a man on a mission to devour my wife.

As I lay back on the cot, I now recalled the first time I noticed Lexi's attitude about Jason had changed. She used to like Jason, but after one of my weekend trips out of town to be with my lover, she seemed to cringe every time I mentioned Jason's name, or whenever he came around.

Their once jovial banter with one another intensified over the years. I brushed it off. Thought they didn't like each other. Lexi, in the end, only tolerated Jason because he was my friend. Someone I thought was my brother.

I felt bad about not seeing those signs. I knew of Jason's reputation with the women. I knew of Jason's hustle mentality. I just never thought he would cheat with my wife or steal from my business. I trusted him with everything. I trusted him with my life. I had to laugh out loud. Because of Jason, life as I knew it was in jeopardy. All because of trusting the wrong person.

My mind went back in time as I recalled a conversation with my father. He'd mentioned that he thought Jason was jealous of me. I didn't want to believe it. Dad even went as far as to say that one day I would regret not heeding his advice.

It didn't happen in my father's lifetime, but it happened, and now my family and I were suffering due to my poor choice of a friend. Unfortunately, we couldn't erase our past. We could only learn from our decisions and try not to make the same mistakes.

I was being selfish for wanting to see Lexi and my children, but seeing them was the only thing keeping me from being depressed. Staring at those four walls day in and day out and listening to the chatter going around in the dorm could drive a man crazy.

I went from never knowing how my day would go to having the

same routine day in and day out. I got up around seven to eat breakfast, or rather play over the food. I showered and most of the
time, it was a cold shower; the hot water hardly ever worked.

I sometimes sat out in the dorm and talked to some of the men
that I had bonded with. I spend the majority of my time in my cell
by myself, reading, doing pushups or sit-ups and sleeping until
mealtime. I repeated the same daily routine. The days were long
and the nights were longer. I marked the dates on the calendar to
keep up with the actual day. Every day seemed the same except
for those times when some of the inmates engaged in fights.

During those times, we went on lockdown. That meant no one
was allowed out of their cells. Fortunately, there were toilets in
each unit so I could not have cared less about leaving the cell unless
it was to head home. Socializing wasn't on my top agenda.

I dozed off. I felt someone's presence in my space and awakened.
It was another inmate. He placed his hand up to his lip to indicate
for me to remain silent. He walked closer as I stood and was on
full alert in case I had to defend myself. I was older than a lot of
the dudes in there, but I was also fit and strong and would have liked
to think that if I had to, I could have knocked another man out.

"I know you didn't kill the guy they are accusing you of killing,"
he whispered.

"Who are you?"

"I'm a friend of the guy who knows who did it."

"Who did it?" I asked.

"I will tell you if you can help my mama get me a lawyer," he
responded.

"How do I know if I can trust you?"

"Because I know you saw the dead body the night before but
didn't call it in. Only two people who would know that would be
you and the actual killer."

He was correct. But I still didn't trust him. However, if he knew something that could help me, it would be in my best interest to pursue it.

"Let's say I made sure your mom had money to get you a lawyer. How are you going to help me?"

"I'm going to get more information from my friend and pass it on to you."

One of the guards came by. "We about to lock the cells. So it's time for you to get to your own cell."

"Man, I was about to beat this old man in some spades."

I played it off. "This young cat doesn't know I'm the king of spades."

"Bet. We'll find out tomorrow," he said, before leaving the cell behind the guard.

CHAPTER 15

Charity

The only thing stopping me from enjoying the relationship with Omar was the fact that Dad was in jail. If it weren't for that, I would've been able to relax and enjoy the times we were spending together.

We were seated across from each other in my kitchen. He was devouring the chicken spaghetti I'd piled on his plate.

"You keep feeding me like this, I'm not going anywhere. Breakfast the other day and then these dinners," he said in between bites.

"I can cook in and out of the kitchen," I joked.

"Yes, you sure can." He wiped his mouth with his napkin.

"Oh, no, please you two, not the kitchen. Is anything sacred around here?" Hope walked in and said.

"Don't hate," Omar teased.

"Please. I'm not trying to get in nobody's relationship right now. Right now I'm doing me."

"Well, Ms. Doing Me, you are welcome to sit and eat with us," I said.

"I'm fixing me a plate and going to my room. Then you two can get back to doing what you were doing. Clean up afterwards, pleaseee."

Hope fixed her plate and left us alone. An hour later, Omar and I were relaxing on the sofa. "Omar, what can you tell me about the Franklin store break-in?"

"Not much to tell. Whoever did it wasn't trying to steal money because they didn't even touch the safe. Whoever did it thinks Mr. Franklin knows something about something."

"I wonder what that is?" I asked, hoping Omar would divulge more information.

"We don't know."

"Do you think it has anything to do with Jason's death?"

"There's a possibility, but I doubt it."

"Why would you say that?" I eased up closer to him.

"The only person Mr. Franklin saw at Jason's was your father."

"Are you sure?"

"According to the report. I'm not going to go with that angle because once I go that route, then my partner and I would be obligated to follow through. I would have to work with the other detectives, and it wouldn't look good for your father."

"Why would you say that? My father had nothing to do with it," I blurted out.

"I know that and you know that, but your father has the money and your brother knows people. The DA could easily say your father paid someone to do it and threaten Mr. Franklin so he won't testify against him."

"Are you serious? Forget I even brought it up then."

"I'm trying to let you see all angles. I'm not trying to make your dad's situation worse."

I wrapped my arm around his neck. "And I appreciate it."

Omar kissed me. "Why don't you let me take your mind off things?"

"You do know how to do that extremely well."

He planted kisses on my neck. I closed my eyes, got up and grabbed his hand. "Follow me to the queendom."

We laughed as we made our way down the hall.

Hope called out, "Glad you're taking it to the room."

Omar and I continued loving on one another until he received an emergency call from his partner. After he left, I found myself lying on my back staring at the ceiling. I could still smell his woodsy cologne lingering in the air. I closed my eyes and dozed off to sleep.

&

The next morning Hope burst into my room. "Did you hear?" she yelled.

"Hear what?"

"Mr. Franklin's dead."

"Are you serious?"

"Yes. He was found at his house. They think it was carbon monoxide poisoning."

"Oh my God." I fumbled in my bed for the television remote and then turned on the news. Hope sat on the edge of my bed.

We watched the morning news until the story was highlighted again. Then the house phone rang.

"It's Mom," Hope said after looking at the caller ID. She answered it. "Yes, Mom. We're watching it now."

Hope hit the speaker button. Our mother's voice rang out from the other end. "Mr. Franklin must've known something. His death can't be an accident like they are making it out to be. Whoever he spotted the night of Jason's murder killed him."

"Maybe it's a coincidence," Hope suggested.

"It's no coincidence," I said. "Omar told me the burglary at Mr. Franklin's store wasn't your normal burglary. The person who destroyed some of the store was trying to send a message."

"Charity, you should have called me when you found that out. I may have been able to convince Mr. Franklin to go stay somewhere else," Mom said.

"She was occupied. She couldn't talk," Hope said.

I rolled my eyes. "I'll call Omar and see what else I can find out."

"Do that, and then call me back. In fact, I'm on my way over there," she said.

Before I could protest, she'd hung up the phone. I looked at Hope. "Good looking out, sis."

"Hey, I'm telling the truth."

"You only tell the truth when it suits you." I dialed Omar's number. He answered. "I was about to call you."

"Have you been up all night?" I asked.

"Yes. Our burglary victim was found dead in his home. We suspect carbon monoxide poisoning but won't know for sure until after an autopsy is done."

"I saw it on the news."

"I will be in touch as soon as I can."

"Mom's on her way over here," I said.

"Okay. Give her my love."

We hung up. Hope was still sitting on my bed. "Do you really think he knew who actually killed Jason?"

"He must have. Why kill him? He saw something and now I'm not sure if we will ever find out what that was."

"Do you trust Omar?" she asked.

"Yes. If I didn't, I wouldn't be spending as much time with him as I have. Do you know of a reason why I shouldn't trust him?"

"No. You seem to be moving a little fast. You're normally the one preaching to me about being responsible. But here you are sleeping with Omar."

"Hope, I've thought long and hard about what I should or shouldn't do with Omar. I've dealt with my past issues with men. I promised myself I was not going to let that affect my dealings with other men and I haven't. Unless Omar gives me a reason not to trust him, we're fine."

"I wish I could feel the same way you do. After Tyler, I don't even want to be bothered."

"You'll get there. Right now, do what you said. Concentrate on you. There's nothing wrong with that. In fact, I encourage you to do so."

"Why? So I can stop being the spoiled brat you think I am?"

"You are spoiled. And you can be a brat."

Hope pouted. "And you can be mean."

"Let me finish. Over the past few months I've seen a change in you. You're not completely there yet, but at least you're concerned about someone else other than yourself. Now come give me a hug. You know I love you."

I got up off the bed and hugged her tight.

CHAPTER 16

Hope

I didn't expect to get all emotional with Charity, but since I'd been on a quest to learn more about myself, I'd decided to be upfront about my feelings with people, and instead of ignoring issues, deal with them.

It was definitely not easy trying to change. I had to first admit to myself I had a very selfish attitude. I was the baby of the family so I was used to getting what I wanted, but maybe I'd taken things a little for granted. In between helping Charity with her business, I'd been reading a lot of self-help books hoping to find one that would help me in my desire to change.

The doorbell rang. Charity beat me to the door. "I got it!"

Mom walked in looking as good as usual. Even under distress she dressed to impress. She wore her signature pearls and was wearing a brown pantsuit.

She hugged us and sashayed right into the living room. She handed Charity the newspaper she'd been holding in her hands. "What did Omar say?"

Charity responded, "He said they are waiting on an autopsy."

"Even if the autopsy comes back as carbon monoxide, it will be because someone initiated it. That means someone knows I stopped by to see him. They also believed he was going to tell me something. I need to get inside of his house."

"Mom, it's not safe to go in his house," I said.

"By now, they've cleared the problem," she assured me.

"Well, I'm not letting you go in there by yourself," Charity said.

"Mom, people recognize you, so you shouldn't be going—period. Not that many would recognize me. I could pretend to be one of his nieces or something. Get inside. Snoop around and see if I can find something."

"But I'm not going to put you in harm's way. Royce would never forgive me if I did. I couldn't forgive myself," she stated.

"We have no choice. If you go, they won't let you in because you're Mrs. Royce Jones. Charity can't go because of Omar."

Charity said, "Mom, she's right. If there's anything in the house, Hope will have to be the one to gain access."

Since that was settled, I got dressed in some skintight jeans and a low-cut blouse. I pulled my hair back with a ponytail. Lately, I hadn't been wearing makeup, but today I decided to get all glammed up.

"Wear this," Charity said as she placed a baseball hat on top of my head.

"You're messing up my look," I said.

Mom said, "No, this is perfect. You want to look like the grieving niece. Let me do a little something here." She used a tissue and smeared some of the mascara around my eyes. I looked like a raccoon.

Charity looked at me. "Now that's perfect."

I shrugged my shoulders. "I'll text you once I'm inside."

"If there's anything to be found, it will be either in the living room or bedroom. Most old people like to keep stuff under mattresses, so check there," Mom said. "Or check on the floor for a loose floor board."

"Be careful, in case you run into Omar," Charity said.

"I've got this," I assured them.

Twenty minutes later, I was on Mr. Franklin's street. There were two police cars parked outside on the curb. I parked behind one of them and walked down the sidewalk toward Mr. Franklin's house.

One of the officers said, "Ma'am, you won't be able to go in. This is a crime scene."

I used some of my acting skills and started crying. "I heard about what happened to Uncle Franklin. I had to come see for myself."

The officer immediately softened his tone. "We're sorry for your loss. Is there someone else you want to call?"

"No, not right now," I said in between sniffles. "Are any of my relatives inside?"

"They were. But they're gone now," the officer responded.

"Do you mind if I go inside? I need to say goodbye in my own way."

"Let me check." The officer went inside and talked to another officer. He came back outside. "We're about through in there, so sure. Come on in."

He held the door open for me. I followed him in. I burst out in tears some more. "You sure you want to do this? Maybe you should come back another time," the officer stated.

"I'm going to be all right," I assured him.

After he went back outside, I walked through the house until I located the room that looked like Mr. Franklin's bedroom. I shut the door and started looking through things. I wasn't exactly sure what I was searching for. Maybe something would stand out, but nothing did. I checked under the mattress like Mom said. Only thing I located under it was a few stacks of money. I left those in place.

I stepped on the floor to see if any of the boards were loose. Nothing. It was a bust.

Something shiny on the floor behind the dresser caught my eye. It was a small video camera. It was too big, however, to fit in my purse. I had to figure out a way to get it out of the house.

I located a small bag in the closet and placed it inside. I walked out into the hallway. I didn't see anyone.

"Ma'am, are you all right," the same officer I'd seen earlier said from behind me. He was back indoors.

"Yes. I didn't realize it was going to be so hard. I need to get out of here." I held the bag in front of me and rushed toward my car.

The officer didn't stop me. I didn't breathe until I was safely inside my car and pulling away. I called Charity. "I'm on my way home."

"Lovie's here. He wasn't too happy about our plan."

"Tell him not to go anywhere. I'll be there in about fifteen minutes," I said.

CHAPTER 17

Lovie

"What were y'all thinking? What if the police figured out Hope wasn't who she said she was? Do you know how that could've hurt Dad's case?" I said as soon as I learned of Mom and my sister's plan.

Charity responded, "Hope should be here any minute." We heard a key in the lock. "In fact, there she is now."

We all looked in the direction of the doorway. Hope rushed in carrying a black bag. She pulled out a small video camera.

"I don't know what's on it, but maybe we can find something."

"Lovie, you're good with those things. See if you can get it to work," Mom said.

I took the camera from her. I hit the *On* button. The red button on it flashed, indicating the battery was low. I opened up the viewing window and pressed *Play*. Nothing was on the video except Mr. Franklin taking footage of his front yard.

"This was a bust," Hope said. "Sorry, y'all."

"Not totally," I proclaimed. "This made me think of something. I don't know why I hadn't thought of it before."

All eyes were now on me. I decided to keep what I was thinking to myself in case it didn't work out.

"Are you going to tell us or what?" Mom asked.

I got up and kissed her on the cheek. "I'll be in touch."

"Lovie, where are you going?" she asked.

"To take care of business."

Hope and Charity had questionable looks on their faces. "Don't do anything else without my knowledge," I said to them as I headed toward the door.

Charity walked behind me. "Lovie, what's up? Come on. You can't keep us all in the dark."

I turned and looked at her. "If I tell you, you'll tell Mom. So until I know what's what, I'm keeping it to myself."

"Fine." She pouted.

"That' s not going to work. Bye, Charity." I left and hopped in my black SUV.

&

I eased my vehicle into the parking lot of what was once Uncle Jason's office. I went inside and the security guard that was normally at the front desk was gone.

"Must be my lucky day," I said to myself as I chose to take the stairway in case the security guard was on one of the elevators.

I only had to go a few stories up before reaching what used to be Uncle Jason's office. I used the key Dad had on his ring and it worked.

For some reason no one had cleared out his office. There were boxes of stuff stacked up, but otherwise, everything else was in place.

I looked through the glass door to see if anyone was coming. I took the liberty of locking the door back. I didn't want the security guard to slip up on me. I went inside of the room where Jason's desk was located.

The drawer to the desk was locked. I removed my pocketknife and used it to break open the lock. I opened up the desk and located some of Uncle Jason's personal information. I flipped through the pages until I located the information I needed. I removed the sheet of paper and placed it in my pocket.

I tried to close the drawer, but it kept hitting something. Frustrated, I pulled the drawer all the way out and a book was squashed. I removed it. I opened it up. It was a ledger. My mouth flew open. I'd hit a goldmine. This had to be the book showing the real amounts of money for some of his clients. It also contained account information and passwords. I'd hit the mother lode. I'd found more information than I'd set out to find.

I closed the desk drawer back up. I wish I had known where his laptop was because that would've helped me as well. I sent Charity a text message asking her for Omar's number. She texted it back to me.

I punched in his number. He answered on the third ring.

"Omar, this is Lovie. How you doing, man?"

"What's up?"

"Do you know where Jason's laptop is? Was it ever recovered?"

"I don't recall seeing it on the list of items. It probably got burned up in the fire," he said.

"Probably," I added. "Thanks. If you find out otherwise, this is my cell number so hit me back."

I ended the call with Omar and now had to get out of the office building without being detected by the security guard. I picked up the book and was about to leave when something told me to check the other desk drawers. I looked through the drawers and saw nothing but files. The last drawer was what I needed. It contained a small computer notebook.

I didn't wait to see what was on it. I grabbed it, along with the book, and left Uncle Jason's office. I locked the door. I chose to use the stairwell again. The security guard was now sitting at the front desk. Instead of going in his direction, I eased down the hall toward one of the side exit doors.

I said a quick prayer and opened the door. There wasn't an alarm. I sighed with relief as I rushed out and to my car. My adventure wasn't over. I eased my car down the alleyway near Uncle Jason's house. The shell of his house still stood.

I parked in the alley and went through the back way. I picked up a huge stick off the ground. I didn't have a problem opening up the back door. It almost fell off the hinges.

I used the stick to move stuff as I rumbled through some of the ashes. I went to the room that used to be his den and didn't locate anything that resembled a laptop. Uncle Jason would have had his laptop at home, so the question I now had was, where was his laptop? If it wasn't in these ashes, then who had it? I walked through the ashes and out the back door the way I had entered. I was careful to make sure no one noticed me.

CHAPTER 18

Omar

The short conversation with Lovie had me wondering a few things. Did the laptop get burned with the rest of Jason's stuff or was it missing in action and the real killer had it? I reviewed the file again to see if I'd overlooked the inventory before, but the laptop wasn't listed.

I pulled up into Jason's driveway and went through the front door and through the ashes. I thought I heard the back door close. I removed my pistol and held it out and went through the rooms until I got to the back door. Nothing. I opened the door and didn't see anything.

I guessed the noise could have been anything. I placed the gun in the holster on my side. I was unable to find any remains of a laptop. I dialed Lovie's number. He answered. He sounded like he was out of breath. "Did I catch you at a bad time?"

"Everything's cool. Just been rushing."

"I double-checked and there wasn't a laptop on the list. I'm at his house now and don't see any remnants of a laptop."

"Whose house?" Lovie asked.

"Jason's," I responded.

"You're at Uncle Jason's house?" he asked.

"Yes. I thought I would come and see if I could locate some of the remains. Just to verify."

"Did you?" he asked.

"Not a thing. So either the laptop got burned to pieces or he didn't have it here."

"That's odd. Because most people carry their laptops everywhere they go," Lovie said.

"True. Do you know where else he would have kept it?" I asked.

"His car. If he didn't have it in the house, he would have kept it in his car."

"Hold on, Lovie." My phone beeped. I answered and then returned to the other line. "I got a call. His car is still in the garage. I'll check it later. It's not going anywhere."

It sounded like I heard Lovie's car screech. I didn't have time to figure it out. I had a call from my partner and needed to get back to the office.

It was close to midnight before my day ended. Charity greeted me at her front door before I could knock.

"You look tired," she commented, after we hugged.

"All I want right now is a long hot bath," I said.

"Already got that covered. Follow me."

I grabbed her hand and followed her to the bathroom. I noticed the bathtub filled with bubbles.

"Everything you need is right here," she said.

Less than an hour later, I was lying next to Charity in her bed. "You're so good to me. I don't know what I did to be blessed with you," I said as I hugged her around her waist and inhaled the strawberry scent of her hair.

"You must have been real good," she teased.

"I talked to your brother," I said.

"Glad one of us did. I hadn't talked to him since he left my house earlier. He was supposed to be following up on something, but he never got back to me about it."

"He's looking for your uncle Jason's laptop. I plan on going back to the house and looking in the garage in his car to see if it's there."

"Why wait? Let's go now," she said.

"Baby, it's after one in the morning. If it's been there all of this time, it'll still be there."

"If Lovie is looking for the laptop, it must be important. I won't be able to sleep knowing it might be there."

"I'll go first thing in the morning."

"But, baby. Please. For me. I'll go with you. I can hold your flashlight."

"Oh, no. I don't want you anywhere near his house. I'll go by myself." I got up and got dressed.

Charity ignored my request. She got dressed, too. "I'm going and there's nothing you can say to change my mind."

"Come on, Bonnie."

"That's right. I'm Bonnie to your Clyde, so let's ride," she commanded.

"Oh, now you want to be a rapper."

I drove over to Jason's house. "Stay in the car. Do not get out. Is that understood," I said to Charity when I pulled up in his driveway.

"I can hold the light," she insisted.

Charity was so stubborn. That was probably her only fault. "Fine. Come on," I said. "But be quiet. We don't want to alert the neighbors."

I held on to one flashlight and handed her another small flashlight I kept for backup. "Stay close behind me," I said.

We made our way into the garage. The car had received some smoke damage. Some of the metal had melted but didn't harm the contents of the car. Looked like the car had been rummaged through. Could have been done by our forensics team.

Charity held the flashlight while I looked in the front and back seats. I had to use force to open up the trunk but didn't locate a laptop.

"Nothing's here. It's possible that the laptop burned up," I said to Charity.

"Let's look one last time," she said.

Against my better judgment, to appease her, I looked again.

I heard sirens. "Charity, I need you to go out back. If you can, meet me in the alleyway. I don't need the officers to see you here with me."

"I'm not going to leave you by yourself. What if they mistake you for a burglar and shoot you. You'll need me here as a witness."

I retrieved my badge from my pocket. "I've got my ID right here. Now go, baby. I would follow you, but my car is parked in the driveway."

I led her to the back door and watched her go out the back gate.

I went back inside and out the front door. I was greeted by two uniformed police officers. "Hold your hands up where we can see them!"

I went through the motions. After they saw my identification, they let me go. I rode around toward the alleyway and picked up Charity.

Charity wrapped her arm around my neck. "I've lost my dad. I can't lose you too," she said.

"Baby, you'll never lose me," I assured her as I drove back to her place.

CHAPTER 19

Lexi

It'd been two months and two days since the ill-fated day Royce had been arrested. Sleep was no longer my friend. I rarely got a full night's sleep. Whenever I could sleep, I welcomed it. I'd dozed off on the couch. When my eyes opened, I didn't expect to see my son, Lovie, asleep in his father's La-Z-Boy.

"Lovie, baby, what are you doing here?"

He yawned. "I came over last night, but you were sleeping so good, I didn't want to wake you. I decided to chill."

"You could've slept in your old bedroom," I said. "You didn't have to stay down here with me."

"I thought it was best," he declared.

"I'm going to go take a shower and cook us some breakfast."

"Mom, you don't have to."

"I feel like cooking and that's exactly what I'm going to do."

Two hours later, we were seated across from each other at the kitchen table eating sausage, grits, eggs and toast.

"Aren't you glad I decided to cook?" I asked Lovie.

"Yes, Mom."

"Now that we're both full, talk to me. Tell me what's going on? You left your sisters' house and I didn't hear from you before falling asleep."

I cleaned up the kitchen as he talked. I listened to him recount the events of the previous night.

"After Omar couldn't find the laptop in Uncle Jason's car, I went back. Something told me to look under the floor boards to see if there was a hidden compartment and there was one in the trunk. Fortunately, the police hadn't looked there."

"So what made you think to look for his laptop?" I asked.

"When Hope brought the video camera, it made me remember Uncle Jason mentioning he had home surveillance set up so he could watch his house when he was at the office."

"I don't recall seeing any cameras," I said. I was washing dishes by hand. I could have used the dishwasher, but washing manually seemed to calm my nerves.

"Me neither, but I recalled him telling Dad that once. I even stopped by his office one day and saw him looking at the monitor from this device."

I listened to Lovie tell me what had happened the day before at Jason's office.

"You should've told me, at least, where you were going. What if the security guard would've caught you? Then I would have to deal with you being locked up too."

"Mom, I was careful. I'm here talking to you now, aren't I?"

"Yes, but—"

"Let's not go there. I need to show you something. I'll be right back."

I finished cleaning up the kitchen as I waited for Lovie to return. He returned with a little laptop computer. I watched as he turned it on and hit a few keys on the keyboard.

"There's no audio on this video, but watch this."

I took a seat and placed it close to Lovie's. The video footage showed Jason going to his door. It showed him talking to someone, but the face of the person couldn't be seen from the angle of the camera. Whomever Jason had been talking to made him upset.

He came back inside, kicking and hitting stuff.

"Keep watching," Lovie said. He pressed a button. The video fast-forwarded.

Someone dressed in all black with a black skullcap covering their face pulled a body into the living room. The person pulled out a gun from their back pocket and then shot the body in the head.

"So he was dead before his body was placed in the living room."

"Exactly," Lovie said. "The person left the room. And then that's when I showed up."

I saw Lovie on the screen. I saw the shock and horror on his face at discovering Jason's body. I watched Royce and I burst through the front door. Although there was no audio, I knew what had taken place next. That's when we all decided to leave and act like we'd never seen anything.

"The person in the black was still in the house when we were there," I said. "And they knew there were cameras because look at them."

"Yes. Whomever it was knew Uncle Jason. Knew him well enough to know he had hidden cameras and knew exactly where they were all located. Because what's not shown is them starting the fire," Lovie said.

"What we need to find out is who that is in the black. I need to call Mitch and see if he can do anything with this footage," I said.

"No, Mom, you can't. If you do that, then you and I could also be arrested. You can't show this to Mitch."

"Who said anything about showing him the entire video? Just enough to show what happened."

"But Mom… Still. He's going to want to know where we got it. How we got it."

"Leave Mitch up to me. Make me a video showing the other part. Maybe if I show him that, he'll see for himself Royce had nothing to do with it, and it'll put some fire up under him to do something.

Because quite frankly, so far, I'm not satisfied on how he's been handling your father's case."

⋙

Later on that day, Lovie dropped off the altered video. "Mom, I hope this helps."

"I hope so too," I agreed. "In the meantime, we also need to figure out who this mysterious person is in the black."

"I'm on it," Lovie declared.

"I didn't bother to tell Hope or Charity what we've found yet. I don't want to chance Charity saying anything to Omar about this," I confessed to Lovie.

"So you don't really trust him either?" Lovie asked.

"It's not that I don't trust Omar. I don't know him well enough. This is my husband's life on the line, and I don't trust anyone but you kids when it comes to his freedom."

Lovie left me alone with my thoughts and the video. I dialed Mitch's number. "Mitch. I have something for you. Can you stop by the house?"

"I'm out of town right now, but will stop by as soon as I get back."

"Out of town? You shouldn't be taking leisure trips while my husband is locked up. What are we paying you for?"

"Lexi, calm down. Royce is my number one client, but I had to do something for another client. I'll be back in the morning and will make sure I stop by there before going home or to the office."

"Fine," I snapped, but wasn't too happy to hear of Mitch's location.

Something was telling me I would need more than this video to free my man. I had to think of something and quick.

CHAPTER 20

Royce

Mitch was seated in the room when the guard let me inside. "I hope you have some good news for me," I blurted. I didn't have time for pleasantries. After being locked up for two months, I was long past small talk.

"Have a seat, Royce; we have a lot to discuss." Mitch opened up his briefcase and took out sheets of paper. "I saw Lexi yesterday."

"How's my wife doing?"

"I thought she was bossy before." He sighed. "Since you've been locked up, she's been relentless. She'll call me until I pick up so I try to answer the first time."

I laughed. "That's my Lexi."

"Lexi showed me a video. The footage shows the real killer pulling Jason's body into the room and then shooting him. I'm obligated by law to show this to the police. I do have a dilemma. If I show it, they'll want to know how I got it and I don't want to pull Lexi into this."

"Then don't share it with them."

"It can prove that you didn't do it," Mitch said.

"I don't want to chance it. I'd rather face the jury without it than have it end up causing legal problems for Lexi."

Mitch slid a brown envelope toward me.

"What's this?" I asked.

"The results you've been waiting on."

The DNA results were back. My hand shook a little as I held

the envelope. I got a paper cut trying to tear it open. I said a silent prayer and pulled the short white sheet of paper out of it.

Tears flowed down my face. The answer I'd been waiting on since finding out Jason had slept with Lexi stared me in the face. There was no more denying the facts.

"Are you okay?" Mitch asked.

I handed him the paper. "Can you arrange a special meeting with Lexi and Lovie? Something like this so I can share this with them in person without the glass dividing us."

Mitch reviewed the results. "I will see what I can do. In the meantime, please reconsider the video. This could really help you."

"I'll think about it."

Mitch left and I was returned to my cell. I had plenty of time to think about the test results. My mind drifted off until I was in a deep sleep. One of the guards came to my cell. He yelled out my name.

"Jones. God must be smiling down on you because you've got a special visit."

I had to pinch myself to prove I wasn't dreaming. I had just spoken to Mitch that morning, so I didn't expect him to get the visitation set up quickly.

"Are you coming or what? This doesn't happen too often so I suggest you hurry it up," the guard said.

He didn't have to tell me again. I jumped off the bunk and followed him to the room where I'd seen Mitch earlier. I inhaled and exhaled a few times. The guard opened the door. Mitch was seated at the table and right next to him were Lexi and Lovie.

Mitch addressed the guard. "I promise you nothing inappropriate will happen. Can you leave us alone for a few minutes?"

"I'm not supposed to. But I can make this exception for Mr. Jones."

I said, "Thank you."

As soon as the door was shut, Lexi hopped out of her chair and we hugged. I hugged her so tightly I didn't want to let her go. I inhaled the mixture of the fruity and floral scent of her perfume. I ran my fingers through her hair. I hadn't touched her hair in over two months. I kissed her lips. I felt the softness of her big brown lips on mine. I'd dreamed of those lips every night. I held her in my arms and squeezed her, never wanting to let go.

Tears flowed down Lexi's face. I wiped her face with one of my hands. "Ooh girl, I've missed you," I said to Lexi.

"I've missed you too, Royce. If you only knew how much."

"I know, baby. Believe me, I know."

Up until this point, no one else had said anything. For a moment, I forgot Lovie and Mitch were in the room.

"Lovie, come give me a hug, son."

Lovie seemed hesitant at first, but obliged me. I hugged him tight too.

Mitch said, "Let's sit before the guard comes back."

I sat down across from Lexi. We held hands. I rubbed her soft hands, loving the feel of hers in mine. "I'm surprised Mitch was able to set this up so fast."

"Someone owed me a favor," Mitch said.

"Thank God for favors." I looked at Lovie and then at Lexi. I pulled out the sheet of paper that held the key to our past and future. "I'm not sure if Mitch told you the DNA test results were back."

Lexi frowned. "No, he did not."

I squeezed her hand. The guard came back in and stood by the door. I wished he would have remained outside a little longer, but I couldn't prolong this another second. In prison, one of the things I'd gotten used to was the lack of privacy.

"Lovie. Lexi, the results show there's a ninety-nine-point-nine percent probability that Lovie—"

"Royce, spill it out. The suspense is killing me," Lexi blurted out.

"Baby, I am." I looked at Lovie. "Lovie, I told you before this test was done that I will always be your dad regardless, right?"

"Yes, sir," he responded.

"Well, the test results show I am your father. So now we have proof that I'm your dad."

"Thank God!" Lexi shouted out.

Lovie sighed heavily. It was as if he had been holding his breath the entire time.

"Dad, you are my father." Lovie got up.

The guard said, "No physical contact."

Lovie sat back down. I placed my hand on top of his. "Son, I knew you were mine. I felt it in my heart. Even if the results had come back different, a piece of paper wouldn't have changed that fact."

Although being behind bars wasn't the ideal situation for me, at that moment in time, I felt joy. Joy that I had my wife and biological son sitting there with me. Love filled the room and filled my heart as I sat there and looked at their beautiful faces. Nothing else right then mattered.

CHAPTER 21

Charity

I ended my phone call with Omar. I got out of my car and walked up the walkway to my parents' house. Hope had ridden over with me, but she was already inside.

"Glad you could finally join us," Mom said as I greeted her and Lovie.

I took a seat on the couch next to Hope.

I saw smiles on their faces. Lovie said, "The DNA results came back and—"

She interrupted Lovie. "Royce is Lovie's father."

I jumped out of my seat and hugged Lovie. "I knew it. See, told you."

Hope hugged Lovie too. "I'm relieved. You would still be our brother, but I couldn't imagine having Jason as a father."

"We saw Royce today," Mom said.

"I wish I would've known; I would've gone with you," Hope said.

"This was a special visit set up by Mitch," Lovie stated. "Dad wanted to tell us the results in person."

Mom stood and paced the floor. "Giving you that good news isn't the only reason why I called you both over here. Mitch informed us after our visit that Royce won't allow him to show him video footage that can clear him so 'operation catch Jason's killer' is still in effect.'"

I looked at Hope and then at Lovie. Hope looked clueless but Lovie... He knew exactly what Mom was talking about.

"I'm missing something," I said. "What video?"

"Lovie and I saw a video of who actually killed Jason, but he had a mask on so we couldn't see his face," our mother said. She went on to give us more details.

"I wish Dad would give Mitch permission to show the police so he could be here with us," I said.

Lovie asked, "Did Omar mention anything about a laptop?"

"Yes. We...I mean *he*, went to look for it but couldn't find it."

Lovie confessed. "I found the laptop in Jason's car. There was a secret compartment in the floor board and I found it."

"That explains it." I shared I'd gone with Omar to look for it and what had happened.

"Charity, don't do anything that stupid again," Mom said. "What if those cops would have burst in on you? You know how trigger-happy some of these cops are. They could have shot you. Or worse, killed you."

"I'm not going to sit and do nothing," I said.

"That's good to know," Lovie said. "Because we will need you to get some information from Omar."

I pulled out my phone. "Sure. What do you need?"

"Put your phone away," Mom said.

Lovie said, "We need for you to get Omar's ID information."

"He keeps it on him or near him at all times," I informed.

Hope said, "We can work together to get it."

Mom said, "She's right. You're smart and you get your good looks from me. Use what your mama gave you."

I would've laughed, but Mom was serious. Lovie added, "We don't need to spell it out to you. You know exactly what we need you to do to get that information."

"Say I do get it. What will you use it for?"

"Don't worry about that now," Lovie said. "Just get it."

Hope and I left and went home. We discussed our plan on the drive home. We were only home a short time when Omar pulled up in his black sports car.

"Perfect timing," he said, as he opened up my door. We kissed.

"I'll see y'all later. I'm going inside," Hope said.

"Hello to you too, Hope," Omar said.

"Whatever," Hope hissed.

I clicked my car alarm. Omar and I walked hand in hand up the walkway. Omar opened the front door and I entered in front of him. I turned around and kissed him. His back hit the door. I stuck my tongue down his throat to let him know I wanted more than a kiss. I wanted so much more.

He moaned. "Where's Hope?"

"I don't know and I don't care," I responded. "Come with me."

We went to my bedroom. I closed the door. We tore each other's clothes off. I pushed him down on the bed. We kissed some more. I planted kisses on his chest. The kisses trailed down to his belly button. I used one hand to unbuckle his pants.

I stared at him. "These need to come off."

Without saying a word, he allowed me to pull off his pants, revealing his boxers. I tossed the pants and boxers to the side of the bed. I stood so he could watch me remove my lace panties.

"You're so beautiful," Omar said.

"And to think it's all yours." I went to the nightstand to remove a condom.

I used my teeth to open the wrapper. Without taking my eyes off Omar, I placed it on top of his long, hard member. I eased on top. "You're so wet," he moaned the moment I sat on top of him.

I rocked back and forth until we both climaxed. I rolled off the top of him. I could feel his breathing slowing down. "Babe, let's go take a shower together," I said.

"What about Hope? You don't want her—"

"Shh. Hope's probably sleep. Come on. Wrap the sheet around you, if you're that self-conscious."

He wrapped the sheet around his body. I pretended to accidentally bump into the table in the hallway. I yelled, "Ouch!"

We continued to the bathroom. I turned on the shower and got in. I looked at Omar, standing there naked. "Are you going to let me get wet all by myself?" I licked my lips as I let the water cascade down my body.

Omar smiled and joined me in the shower. He lifted me and positioned me so that we were making love. I was so caught up in the moment that I didn't realize we were doing it bareback until I felt his hot, wet sperm fill me up.

He moaned in pleasure and I cried out *"No"* inwardly.

CHAPTER 22

Hope

Charity's room looked a mess. Her clothes were mixed up with Omar's. His pants were thrown on the opposite side of the bed. I left the bedroom door open so I could hear when the water stopped.

I searched through his pants and located his wallet. I found a card that had his information and took a picture of it with my phone. I forwarded the picture to Lovie via text and placed it back in the wallet. Since I was being nosy, I looked through some of his pictures to make sure he didn't have pictures of another woman. I saw a much younger picture of him that looked familiar. I recalled seeing the picture somewhere else, but couldn't think where.

I heard the water turn off. I placed the picture back in the wallet and stuffed the wallet back in his pants pocket. I threw the pants back on the side of the bed.

I heard the door creak, which meant the bathroom door was opening. I couldn't panic. I had to think of something quick. I tried to roll under the bed, but couldn't. I ran to the closet door and shut it just in time; by now they were in the room.

I used the light from my cell phone so I could find a comfortable place to sit. Unless Omar went home, I would be spending the night in the closet. I heard Charity say, "Do you want something to drink?"

Omar responded, "A cold bottle of water would be nice."

"I'll be right back."

I knew she was going to look for me. I hope she didn't think I had up and disappeared. It sounded like Omar was on the phone.

"I'm not at home... No, she has no idea and I plan on keeping it that way."

I wished I could've heard whom he was talking to.

"Look. I can't talk now. I've told you I will call you. You never know who's around and I can't risk it."

I knew it. He wasn't the honest man he claimed to be. He was cheating on my sister. I couldn't wait to bust him. I almost burst out the closet but stopped before opening the door.

In his pants pocket not only did I find his wallet, but his gun and with me bursting out of the closet, I didn't want to risk him shooting me by mistake. Instead, I was stuck in the closet. I heard Charity's voice.

"Here's your water."

"What's wrong?" Omar asked her.

"Nothing. Well, at least I hope it's nothing," she responded.

"Look in the closet," I wanted to scream, but instead, I removed some of her sweaters, placed them on the floor and used them as a pillow. Every time I closed my eyes, I heard the bed screeching or moans. Falling asleep wasn't going to be easy.

ð

I wasn't sure of when I dozed off. The next morning, I heard my name called.

"Hope," Charity said.

The light was on. Charity stood above me. "Hey. You alone?"

"I am now. You've been in here all night?" Charity asked.

"Duh. Didn't you come look for me after your sexcapade?"

"Yes, but when I didn't see you, I assumed you left."

"My car was outside," I stated as I stood. I rubbed my butt. "I need a massage after sleeping on that hard floor."

"You should have texted me."

"I didn't want him to see the text," I admitted.

"It doesn't matter now. You're here. You're okay."

"I will never ever watch a porn tape. Hearing you and Omar go at it how many times last night was enough for me."

Charity blushed. "He does have a healthy appetite."

"I did overhear something when you went to get something to drink that you should look more into."

"What's that?" Charity asked.

I glanced around her room and saw clean bedding was in place. "Glad to see you changed the sheets on your bed."

"Whatever. What did you overhear?"

"I couldn't tell who he was talking to, but he seemed secretive. I don't know if it was another woman or not."

"He could have been talking to his partner. They are working on multiple cases."

"If you say so," I uttered.

"Forget that nonsense. Did you get a copy of his ID so Lovie can have it?"

"Yes. I've already texted it to him."

"Good. In the meantime, I need for you to help me with this luncheon today."

"I absolutely forgot," I stated.

❧

Two hours later, I was assisting Charity at the luncheon for twenty people in one of the local hotel conference rooms.

Charity and I stood in the doorway. She smiled. "Another satisfied customer."

"I heard from Lovie. After we finish here, he wants us to stop by the funeral home," I said.

"Wait a minute," Charity said.

"What?"

"I think I just saw Omar."

I followed Charity down the hall. "Omar," I heard Charity call out.

Omar stopped right before getting on the elevator. He turned around. "Charity, what are you doing here?"

"She wants to know why you're here," I said.

Charity looked at me. "Hope, I've got this."

"Are you working?" Charity asked.

"Uh...sort of."

"It's either yes or no," Charity said. By now, she had her arms folded.

Omar grabbed her by the arm and led her off to the side so I wouldn't be able to hear their conversation.

I stood nearby. I strained my ears to hear, but I could only make out bits and pieces of their conversation. Charity walked by me. "Come on, let's go."

I ran up behind her. "Why is he here?"

"He's undercover and he claims I almost blew his cover."

"That's bull. I bet you he was going to get under some covers."

"Hope, I don't want to hear your theories. Every man is not a dog like Tyler."

"I'm just saying. First, the phone call and now he's here at a hotel. Come on, Charity, you're supposed to be the smart one."

"Hope, we can talk about this later. You're making a scene."

I didn't realize I was talking loud. I was frustrated. For her sake, I hoped Omar was nothing like Tyler.

CHAPTER 23

Lovie

I sat outside of the Bottom's Up Club. Slim had gone inside. I'd told Hope and Charity to meet me at the funeral home, but in the meantime, I needed to confirm something with Slim.

I greeted some of the fellows as I made my way toward Slim. He was posted in his usual spot with his regular entourage.

"Look who finally had time to join us," Slim said. He stood and gave me a brotherly hug. "Sit down. Have a drink on me."

"I'm simply passing through. I wanted to holla at you for a minute."

Slim looked at the people around him. "Give us a few minutes. First round of drinks are on me."

They cheered as they left us alone.

I sat down in the empty chair next to him.

"Any word yet?" I asked.

"Nothing. Quiet as a mouse."

"Maybe you can help me. Does this look like anybody you know?" I handed him my cell phone, showing a still shot of the person who dragged Jason's body.

"Naw, man. Check this out. That's an expensive watch. None of these other cats would be sporting it." He pointed at the watch on the picture. Slim kept talking. "Those aren't no regular gators he got on. Those are custom made. So whoever this is, he got money. Not a dude from off the street."

"Thanks for checking it out for me," I said. Slim had made some good points. But it didn't narrow down who could have killed Jason.

"You know anything I can do to help you, I will."

I stood. "I have funeral home business to attend to. I'll be seeing you around."

"Bet...take care and tell your pops I said hello. I got my boys looking out for him. So you don't have to worry about nobody messing with him on the inside."

I left out the club and drove straight to the funeral home. The family was seated in the office chatting when I walked in.

"I see business is good," Mom said as she scrolled through something on my computer.

"Business couldn't be better," I confirmed.

We talked about funeral home business while Charity and Hope bickered about something.

"You two need to chill with whatever y'all got going on," Mom said.

Hope stuttered, "Yes, ma'am."

She looked at me. "Lovie, you called this family meeting. What do you have for us?"

I sat on the corner of the desk. "I've discovered whoever killed Jason isn't some thug off the street. I also found some of Jason's hidden accounts where he'd stolen some of his clients' money and placed it in Swiss bank accounts."

"Wow. So what are you going to do with the information?" Charity asked.

"I'm going to be the Black Robin Hood and return the money to its rightful owners," I responded.

Hope said, "Wait. Maybe we should take a vote on this."

Lexi said, "There's nothing to vote on. That's not Jason's money and it's definitely not our money. Lovie is right. It needs to go to the rightful owners."

We all looked at Hope who looked away. "I told y'all I'm trying to change. I'm not quite all the way there yet, okay?"

"Thanks to Hope, I got my boy to access the files at the police department. One thing your man forgot to tell us, Charity, is that without the weapon, the DA's case is still a little weak. So with my DNA coming back proving Dad is my biological father, he might become a free man after all."

"But the jury can still convict," Charity said.

"They're not supposed to if the evidence doesn't show he did it," I stated.

"I'm not taking anything for chance. Since the police have stopped looking for Jason's killer, it is up to us to find out who this mystery guy is. We find him. We're able to free your father, clearly, without any suspicions or doubts."

"I agree," I said. "Mom, I got you Jason's secretary's information."

"Good. I'm going to pay her a visit. She left town for a reason and she's going to tell me why."

"One of us should go with you," Hope said.

"If you can wait until Monday, I can get someone to handle things here and I can go."

"Charity can go with me," Mom stated.

"Mom, his secretary was always flirting with me. You can come off a little strong. You'll need me there to be a buffer. Trust me," I suggested.

"Fine. Lovie, you handle things here and we'll be making a day trip to Alexandria."

They left the office. I stayed behind. With working at the funeral home and trying to decipher files and information, I hadn't had time to let it sink in that Royce Jones was indeed my biological father. I had to admit that I had been a little scared the tests would come back differently. I was glad all of my fears were for naught. Having that creep's blood running through my veins would have made me go mad, I was sure.

I pulled up the still picture of the man who had killed Jason and zoomed in. Those eyes staring back at me looked familiar, but I couldn't place them. As energy depleted as I was, I would not be going to sleep early that night. Instead, I would be cross-referencing Jason's clients with photos, trying to see if I could locate those same piercing eyes that stared at me from the still photo.

It was after midnight when I left the funeral home. I turned down all of the lights and drove home. I was like the walking dead as I turned the knob on my front door. My eyes widened at the sight of seeing my entire place ransacked.

I went through the apartment and saw that my bedroom was in just as bad a shape as the living room. I dialed Omar's number.

CHAPTER 24

Lovie stood in the doorway as I surveyed his ransacked apartment. "Is anything missing?"

"All of my electronic equipment's still here. They didn't find my secret stash. That's why I called you and not the other police. Somebody's looking for something. They think I have something that I don't have."

"Did you ever find the laptop?" I asked.

"I was going to ask you the same question," Lovie responded.

"I'm surprised Charity didn't tell you about our adventure at Jason's house."

"She told me about it. I didn't know if you'd had a chance to look again."

"Yes, but I came up short. I really want to find that missing laptop myself." I looked around some more, walking from room to room. "If nothing's missing, there's really no sense in filing a report."

"I'm good. I'll have one of my lady friends straighten this up for me. I'll keep it moving. I'm waiting on a locksmith so I can get the locks changed," Lovie told me.

"That's a good idea. I suggest moving your secret stash too, just in case whoever did this comes back."

"I'm already ahead of you." Lovie walked me to the door.

"If you find out who did this, let me know. Don't try to play payback. Let me handle it," I said as I turned to face him. Lovie remained quiet. "I'm serious. Charity would never forgive me if I let something happen to her brother."

"I can't make any promises. But if I find out who did it and you can get to them first, you're welcome to do your thing. If I find them first, well, let's just say, your services won't be needed."

"I'm going to pretend like I didn't hear that," I uttered as I left and went to my car.

I wanted to see Charity, but it was late. I needed to clear things up from earlier. I pulled her number up on my phone. I started to hit the Call button but changed my mind. I wouldn't be selfish. I could wait until the next day.

I went inside my lonely apartment, poured a beer and sat on the couch. I flipped the stations and landed on ESPN and watched the sports highlights until I fell asleep.

ॐ

"For a cop, you sure don't keep your place secure," a loud voice with a lot of bass said.

"What in the world?" I jumped up out of my sleep.

Slim sat in a chair next to the couch. "Rise and shine. It's after eight."

"Slim, what are you doing here...in my apartment?"

"I came to collect on a debt."

"I thought I'd taken care of that debt."

"Consider what you did a down payment. You wouldn't be in the position you're in if it wasn't for me."

"Slim, I got your evidence moved. You're a free man. What else do you want from me?"

"I want you to keep an eye out on my boy."

"Who and why?" I asked.

"You're dating his sister and why...well, that's for me to know and you to not worry about."

"Does Lovie know about your shady business practices?" I asked.

"Everyone knows what I do. I'm not worried about Lovie. He's loyal. He's not a snitch. What I'm concerned with is making sure he doesn't tie his dad's situation up with any business you and I have going on."

"Slim, I've told you this before. What happened to Jason has nothing to do with you. So as far as I'm concerned, there's no need for me to watch Lovie. Lovie's harmless."

Slim blew smoke in my face. "And I want you to make sure it stays that way. Lovie's my boy and I would hate for anything to happen to him because of you."

"Nothing's going to happen to him. Not unless you or one of your men do something."

"Lovie has a free pass out on these streets," Slim said. "But you, the verdict is still out."

"Slim, I don't hang out with Lovie like that, but I'll do my best to make sure he never finds out you and I know each other."

"As long as you do, our relationship is still intact. Have a good day, Detective." Slim placed the burning cigar in the ashtray on my coffee table. He left without saying another word.

I clenched my fists. I was frustrated. I must have forgotten to lock my door when I had come in the night before. Slim was the last person I wanted to see. We'd met some years ago. Back then I wasn't on the right side of the law. I'd just moved to town on a quest to learn something about my past. During that quest, I needed some quick money and Slim provided that outlet.

When I decided to get out of the game and go legit, Slim threatened to kill me because I knew too much about his operation. I convinced him that it was a good idea to have someone on the inside of law enforcement. As long as I kept feeding him information to help him stay out of major trouble, the easier my life was.

He wasn't too happy about his last situation because while I was trying to advance from street cop to detective, several drug bust operations went down without my knowledge. Slim blamed me for his arrest because I didn't warn him and ever since then, things had been tense between us.

I was sick and tired of being beholden to Slim. My plans were to eventually go work for the Feds and get out of the area. I'd come too far to let Slim stop me so, in the meantime, I pacified him by handling small requests.

I needed to get Slim out of my mind and concentrate on Charity. I couldn't have her mad at me. After I showered, I planned on making a morning stop, but first, I needed to pick up some flowers. With flowers and my kilowatt smile, she couldn't do anything but forgive me.

CHAPTER 25

Lexi

Lovie drove us to Alexandria, located in central Louisiana, without incident. His GPS system directed us to the address we had for Jason's ex-secretary.

The house wasn't new, but it was nice in a well-kept area and looked like it had a freshly groomed yard. Beautiful multiple colors of rose bushes lined up around the house.

Lovie pulled up behind a late-model luxury car.

"Mom, let me do most of the talking," Lovie said, right before we exited.

I ignored him. I checked out our surroundings as we walked up the driveway and onto the front porch.

I stood behind Lovie. He rang the doorbell. An elderly woman opened the door.

"May I help you?" she asked.

Lovie said, "Yes. I came to see Diana."

"She didn't tell me she was expecting company," the elderly woman stated.

"I was in town and wanted to surprise her," Lovie said.

"And who is this?" The woman pointed at me.

"This is my mom."

I walked around Lovie and extended my hand. "Hi. How are you?"

The elderly woman shook my hand. "I guess it's okay if you come in. My niece is in her room. I'll tell her you're here."

We followed her inside. The house smelled like lemon Pine-

Sol. The elderly woman was probably responsible for keeping it clean. She led us to the living room.

"You have a nice place," I said.

"Thank you. My husband bought this for us, but he's since gone on to glory."

"Sorry to hear that."

"Don't be. Laurence and I lived a full life. We were married fifty years. He was suffering in the end. Death brought peace for the both of us."

I looked at Lovie. Lovie looked at me. We took a seat on the couch.

The elderly woman stopped and turned around. "Where are my manners? I forgot to ask you if you wanted anything to drink or snack on?"

"We're fine," I responded. "Thank you."

"Young man?" she addressed Lovie directly.

Lovie responded, "Yes, we're fine."

"Okay. If you change your minds, let Diana know. I'll go get her for you now."

A few minutes later, Diana, dressed in a sundress and sandals, walked in the room. Our backs were to her so when she walked in front of us and saw our faces, she turned pale.

"What...what are you doing here?" Diana stuttered.

Lovie spoke first, "Diana, hi. We were passing through and wanted to check on you."

I added, "You know after everything that happened with Jason and all."

"But...but how did you find me?" she asked. She fell down into the chair.

I allowed Lovie to speak for now. "It was easy. We knew it must be hard on you, losing Uncle Jason."

I listened to Lovie try to soften her up and act all concerned.

"And we wondered why you left town so suddenly. Did someone threaten you?" I asked. I was getting tired of the pleasantries.

"No... no...why would you say that?" Diana asked.

"After Jason's funeral, you disappeared," Lovie responded.

"I tried to find work there, but couldn't," she stated. "Besides, the police say Mr. Jones killed Jason. That's why I'm surprised you're here."

"Royce had nothing to do with Jason's death. The way your hand is shaking, you know it as well as we do," I said.

Her face turned beet red. "It's time you leave."

I moved to the edge of my seat. I looked back to make sure her aunt wasn't nearby. No sense in making her nervous. "Look here, little girl. You don't understand who you're messing with. I'm not one to be toyed with. If you know something, you better tell me, or you will regret it."

"I told you I don't know anything. And I really would like for you to leave."

"Lovie, deal with her, because I can't. I'm going to find me a bathroom. I need to release my bladder."

I left the two of them in the living room. I didn't have to use the bathroom, but I did need to locate the room where Diana was staying. I wandered through the house and located what looked like could have been her room. I opened the purse sitting near the bed and looked in the wallet. Jackpot.

Since I confirmed it was her purse, I went through the purse and opened up her checkbook. My eyes widened when I saw weekly deposits of one thousand dollars. Who was Diana working for to make that amount of money as a secretary? Or was the deposit hush money?

Yes, Diana knew more than what she was saying. I tore off one of her blank deposit slips so I would have her account number and placed the paper in my bra.

I didn't find anything else in her purse. I located her cell phone sitting on the nightstand next to her bed. I picked it up. Fortunately for me she didn't have a code on it. I scrolled through her call log. A number kept coming up private. I had to hurry up. I put the phone down. Then I thought about her contacts. I picked the phone back up and located the contacts icon and clicked on it. I scrolled through. There was an entry with the name Private. I opened it up. The number was a Shreveport number. I recited the number out loud and made a mental note of it so I could write it down later. I hoped I didn't forget it.

I placed the phone back on her bed. I turned to leave, but the picture on her dresser caught my attention. I walked over to it and picked it up. It was a picture of her and Jason. Looked like they were on an island. They looked like more than boss and employee. Jason and Diana had been lovers.

CHAPTER 26

Royce

The young man whom I'd ensured Mitch also defended came into my cell holding a deck of cards. We set up a game as a guise as we talked.

"Mr. Jones, you're going to think I lied, but I didn't. I wanted to show you something."

He handed me a newspaper clipping. I read it. "Who is this?"

"This is the man who knew about what happened to the man you're accused of killing."

The article stated the man was murdered while walking down the street. The assailants were unknown. Witnesses stated that a dark-colored car rolled up on the man and the passenger rolled down their window and shot multiple times. The man died on the scene.

"I'm afraid they may know that I'm on to something. My friend never told me who actually did it. He was going to visit me this week. I was supposed to get more details then."

"I'm sorry to hear about your friend. I really don't want others getting killed behind all of this."

"Mr. Jones, if you want to cancel the lawyer, I understand."

"No. You were doing your part. So Mitch is still your attorney. But there is one thing you can do to make this up to me?"

"What? I'll do anything," he said.

"Get your life together. Don't do anything else to end up back here."

"But it's hard for a brother like me to get a job; especially with a record. I hustle to eat."

"If Mitch is able to get you out of here, I can guarantee you a job. But I need for you to promise you will stop selling drugs."

"You can? At your funeral home?" he asked.

"Yes. I can train you as a pallbearer. Well, since I'm locked up here, I wouldn't be training you. But I will have one of my men train you. But all of this depends on you. Is this something you would be interested in?"

"Yes, sir. Not that I understand anything about working around dead bodies. But if the pay is good, count me in."

"I'm not going to mislead you. You're not going to make as much money as you would if you were hustling, but I pay fair."

The young man looked up in the air as if he was thinking. "If it'll keep me off the streets and not back here, I'll do it."

"Great. Then we have a deal." I reached across the cards and shook his hand.

"Lights out," a guard's voice was heard over the intercom.

The young man gathered up the cards and left my cell. A few minutes later, the cell doors closed and I heard the loud clicking noise securing the door.

I was disappointed in learning of his friend's death for several reasons and mainly a selfish one. He could have been holding the key to who had actually killed Jason and that information could have freed me.

I tossed and turned the majority of the night. I woke up in a cold sweat. Darkness filled the room. The dim light from the center of the dorm was the only thing that stopped it from being pitch black.

My heart rate increased at the thought of never going home. I thought about the video Mitch now had. I was beginning to have second thoughts about it. Maybe I should let him submit it to the police. Maybe they could use it to identify who the person was. I needed Mitch to show me the video. Maybe I could identify who the person was.

Morning couldn't come quick enough for me. I never did fall back to sleep. I was fortunate to be one of the first men in the shower so I could get some hot water for a change.

"Jones, you ain't got all day," one of the guards yelled, as I hurried up and showered.

After dressing back in the same orange jumpsuit, I went to the phone. There wasn't a line. I called Mitch first, but didn't get an answer. I dialed Lexi's number.

"Baby, it's so good to hear your voice," I said.

"Sorry I missed visitation. But I had good reason," Lexi said.

"What's going on?"

"Lovie and I went to Alexandria. We paid Diana a popup visit yesterday. I think she knows more than what she's telling."

"Babe, don't say anything else. They may be taping our conversation."

"You're right. I keep forgetting that."

"Alexandria? What is she doing there?"

"She was shocked to see us. But don't worry, dear. I'll write you. You know the drill."

That meant she would give the letter to Mitch to give to me. That way I would know no one else had read it.

"How are the kids?" I asked.

"They're doing fine. Charity's still seeing that cop."

"Omar Underwood?"

"Yes. Mr. Omar. I like him, but under the circumstances, I don't know if she should be dating him."

"Has he given you a reason not to trust him?" I wasn't too keen on her dating anyone, especially after the last two boyfriends she'd had. Both of those men ended up hurting her. I couldn't bear to see my baby girl in pain.

"He's been great. I'll fill you in when I write you."

Lexi and I talked for a few more minutes and then had to hang up. It wasn't that we wanted the call to end; the operator interrupted us. "You have fifteen seconds left on this call."

We said, "I love you" to one another and the call disconnected. I felt a little better after speaking to Lexi.

"Jones, we need you back in your cell," one of the guards yelled at me.

I rushed back to my cell but not without seeing them carry out the young man whom I'd been talking to the night before on a stretcher.

"What happened?" I asked one of the other inmates.

"Somebody shanked him."

Shanked meant someone had used a homemade weapon and stabbed him. Whoever did it thought he had revealed something to me. From now on, I would have to watch my back. Danger was all around me.

CHAPTER 27

Charity

I slipped away from Omar long enough to meet up with my family. Ever since I'd seen Omar at the hotel, he'd gone out of his way to make sure I knew he was not seeing anyone else. It was to the point where I felt like he was smothering me. He was overcompensating so I tried not to complain.

I poured myself a glass of juice and returned to the living room in my parents' house. My siblings were all seated as well.

Mom cleared her throat. "As you girls know, Lovie and I went to Alexandria yesterday and met up with Diana."

"She acts like she's in hiding, so we know she knows more about what happened than she's telling anyone," Lovie said.

Hope and I listened to our mom explain to us what had happened while they were visiting Diana. I wasn't too surprised to hear that she and Jason were having an affair.

"Lovie's trying to find out who has been making, or has made, deposits into her account."

"I'm so glad this is almost over," Hope said.

"We hope it's over," Lovie said. He looked down at his cell phone. A few seconds later, he said, "Y'all will never believe this."

"What?" I asked. My cell phone alerted me I had a text. I knew it was Omar.

"Someone has been making transfers from one of Jason's accounts. So someone else besides me knows his account information," Lovie said.

"The plot thickens," Mom said. "I need a TracFone. I got this number off Diana's phone. This person may be the one using Jason's account. I don't want to call it from either one of our phones, though."

Lovie stood up. "I've got you covered. I have one in the trunk of my car."

"I'm not going to even ask you why you're riding around with a TracFone."

"It's best you don't," he said before leaving out to get the phone.

"I spoke with your dad today. He sends his love," she shared with us.

"I miss him so much," Hope said.

Mom squeezed in between us. She placed one arm around Hope and the other around me. "You girls are so strong. I'm proud of how you're stepping in and doing whatever needs to be done to keep this family together."

"You're our example," I said.

She kissed me on the cheek.

Lovie walked back in holding the phone. "What's the number?"

Mom remained sitting between the two of us. She recited a number. Lovie dialed it and placed the call on speaker. An automatic voice stated, "The person you're trying to call…"

"That must be the wrong one. I wrote it down. I'll be right back." She got up and left the living room.

Lovie said, "Charity, what's up with you and Omar?"

Hope cleared her throat. I gave her that "don't say anything" look.

"Omar and I are just fine. He treats me nice and that's all I'm concerned with."

"I still have my reservations about him," Lovie said.

"Why? I don't understand. He's been helping. And although you haven't told Mom or us, I heard about your place being ransacked. You called him about it, so you realize he's trustworthy."

"And that needs to stay between us. Mom has no idea it happened," Lovie said.

Mom walked in on the tail end of our conversation. "Are y'all keeping secrets from me?"

Hope intervened. "We were planning to take you out to dinner at your favorite restaurant, but somebody forgot to make the reservations."

Hope looked at me and then at Lovie.

Lovie said, "Guilty. It's my fault. You know with my schedule, I've gotten a little forgetful."

I played along with the charades. "But we can still go out."

"I'm not sure if I'm up to it." She handed Lovie a piece of paper before sitting down.

Mom was clearly in a slump because she loved to go out. Since the incident with dad she rarely went out.

Lovie dialed the number. The call went to voicemail. "All I can do now is wait for the person to call back or try the number again later."

I said, "We're all dressed for the occasion. Let's at least go to Copeland's or Longhorn Steakhouse."

"I'm not sure," Mom pondered.

Lovie pulled on her hand. "Come on, Mom. What's something you always say?"

Hope answered, "You can never keep a good woman down."

I said, "And we're the Joneses. No matter what happens. Good or bad, we stick together."

Lovie added, "And we don't hide our heads in the sand, so stand strong and tall and keep it moving."

Our mother laughed. "I need to stop giving you my pep talks.

Y'all are using my words against me. Okay. Fine. Let me freshen up and we can go to Copeland's. I haven't had any oysters in a long time."

"Hope and I will ride together and you and Lovie can meet us there. I can call Omar to see if he wants to meet us there."

All eyes were on me. Mom said, "Dear, don't. This is a family dinner. For now, I want to be with my three kids. Omar being there would make it a little awkward."

I honored her wishes. I sent Omar a quick text alerting him I was going to dinner with my family. Our date night would have to be postponed until another night.

"So what did Omar say?" Hope asked.

"Nothing. We'll hook up later. He knows how important my family is to me," I responded.

I wondered why Hope thought Omar would have a problem with me hanging out with my family. I shrugged it off for the moment.

CHAPTER 28

Hope

Charity pulled up in the full parking lot of Copeland's at the same time Lovie did. We all walked inside together.

"Table for four," Mom told the greeter.

"Right this way." The greeter led us to a table near the center of the room.

Mom asked, "Do you have another table? I would like something not so out in the open."

"Sure. Follow me," the woman said.

We followed her to a table that was to the left of us.

We took a seat. She handed us each a menu. "Your waiter will be with you in a minute to get your drink orders."

"Did you see the way some people were looking at us when we walked in?" Mom asked.

"No, I wasn't paying them any attention," I responded.

"Mom, you're being paranoid," Lovie said.

"I don't think so. Ever since your dad got arrested, people have been acting funny with me."

"What's one thing you've drilled into our heads growing up?" Charity asked.

I responded for her. "If they are acting funny with you, they weren't really your friends to start off with. So why care—"

"Wait until you have kids and they start using your own words against you."

We all laughed.

A waiter stopped by our table and took our drink orders.

"I already know what I want. What about you all?" Mom asked.

"I'm not sure," I responded.

"Let's start off with an appetizer then," Lovie said.

The waiter took our drink and appetizer order.

"I need to go to the ladies room. I'll be right back," I said.

I got up and located the restroom. On my way back to my seat I heard a familiar voice call out, "Hope. Hope Jones."

I turned around and came face to face with a guy I'd had a serious crush on in high school. "Raymond. How are you?"

Raymond walked up to me and gave me a tight hug. The woman he was with didn't seem too happy. She frowned. "I've been asking about you, but no one seemed to have your new number."

"What's your number? I'll call you and you can lock it in."

I pulled out my cell phone. Raymond recited his number. I called it and he locked my number in. The woman he was standing with walked out the door.

"I don't think your date was too happy about that," I said, looking in the direction of the door.

"She'll be all right. But hey, let me go. Hope, it was good seeing you. Don't put me on your 'don't answer list' because I will be calling."

"Do that. Maybe we can get together for coffee or something."

"I've moved back so we have a lot of catching up to do," he said.

His cell phone started ringing. He glanced down. "That's my date. Call you later, Hope." He hugged me. "Again, good seeing you."

"Good seeing you too." I watched Raymond walk away before heading back to my table.

"I see you ran into Raymond. How is he?" Mom asked.

I sat down. "He's fine."

Charity responded, "Yes, real fine."

Lovie grunted. "Look. I don't want to hear y'all talk about men like they are pieces of meat."

"Why not, dear? Men do it about women all of the time," Mom said with a grin covering her face.

An hour later, we were all full from our meals. Mom said, "Kids, I don't know what I would do without the three of you. You've helped me deal with this ordeal."

"Lexi, where have you been hiding?" one of Mom's friends with an irritating voice sounding like a screeching cat said.

Mom stood and greeted her with a hug and air kiss. "Darla, I've been around."

"We miss you at our monthly luncheons."

"I'm sure you have. You've missed me so much you haven't bothered to call," Mom noted.

The smile on Darla's face left. She started stuttering, "We... didn't want to...intrude."

Mom sat back down. "Well, dear. As you can see, I'm out with my three lovely kids. You're sort of intruding right now."

"I'm so sorry. Call me next week. Maybe we can do brunch," Darla said before leaving.

Mom said when she was sure Darla wasn't in earshot, "And maybe not. Her and the rest of that crew are so fake. None of them have called to see how I was doing. I'm through with all of them. They all can kiss my—"

"Mom," Lovie interrupted.

"Well, you know what... they can kiss my you know what," she said, right before downing another glass of red wine.

The rest of the night went by without anything dramatic happening. When we got home, Charity went to her room so she could talk to Omar in private. I went to my room because after eating such a huge meal, I was sleepy.

I dressed for bed and got under the covers. My cell phone beeped, alerting me to a text message. It was Raymond.

"Are you still up?" he asked.

I typed my response: Yes

A few seconds later, my phone rang. It was Raymond. "I hope I'm not interrupting anything," he said.

"Being that I'm single, no, you didn't."

"Got the answer to one of my questions." I could hear the joy in his voice.

"Did you get rid of your date?"

"For the record, she was just a date. She is not my girlfriend. I'm currently single as well."

"Oh, okay." I had to admit I was happy to hear that. The old me wouldn't have cared if he had a girlfriend or not. I usually went after who and what I wanted regardless. The new me, however, was trying to be different. I was trying to be considerate. If he'd told me that was his girlfriend, I would've respected their relationship. But since he'd confirmed she wasn't, I considered forgetting about my hiatus from men. Seeing Raymond had stirred up some things in me that I'd thought died with Tyler.

CHAPTER 29

Lovie

I had to lie about why I wanted to stay in my old room. Well, it wasn't a complete lie because with everything going on, I felt more comfortable staying with Mom. I didn't want her staying in that big two-story house by herself; especially after what had happened to my place.

I walked through all of the rooms downstairs and double-checked to make sure the windows were secure and that the alarm was set. I didn't expect to see Mom sitting at the kitchen counter sipping from a bottle of vodka.

I took it away from her. "Mom, I'm worried about you. You know how you used to get on Dad about all of the drinking. Well, I think you're drinking a little too much."

"I don't have the strength to argue with you." She got out of the chair and almost tumbled. I grabbed her before she could fall.

"Come on. Let me help you back upstairs."

"Lovie, if Royce doesn't come home, I don't know what I will do. I miss him so much," she slurred.

"I know you do. We all miss him."

"I haven't always been the perfect wife and your dad hasn't always been the perfect husband, but we were perfect for each other. Why me? Why is this happening? Why? Why? Why?" she said over and over.

"Mom, it could have happened to anyone. But we're dealing with it. And Dad will be back home with us…with you before too long." I tried to assure her, but I wasn't so sure of it myself.

By now, we were in her room. I led her to the bed. I turned down the comforter and gently gave her a shove so she fell on the bed.

"I don't know what I did to be blessed with a son like you. You're always taking care of your mama."

"I always will," I declared. "Now get under the covers and go to sleep. I'll be in my room, if you need me."

"Give Mama a hug."

I gave her a hug. I could smell the alcohol. "Goodnight, Mom," I said.

"Goodnight, Lovie."

The moment her head hit the pillow she was out cold.

I tiptoed out of the room and shut the door.

I walked down the hallway to my former room. It still had a masculine look, decorated in dark green and dark brown. I eased out of my clothes until I was down to my boxers. I hopped on top of the bed and started texting some of my female friends. I wasn't trying to be with anyone serious, but I needed a distraction.

One was upset at me for not returning her calls. I told her good-night quick; I wasn't in the mood to argue. The other wanted me to know she had completely cleaned my apartment. I promised to treat her to a nice dinner. She'd already retrieved the money I had left for her in an envelope on the counter.

Bored texting, I turned the light out and got under the covers. I drifted off to sleep. The phone rang. I reached for my cell phone. Nothing. I heard the ring again. It wasn't my cell phone. It was the other phone. I located it and hit the *On* button.

"Hello," I said.

"Who is this?" the muffled voice asked from the other end.

"You called my number. So who are you?"

"Must be a wrong number," the muffled voice responded.

"Must be," I stated.

I looked at the caller ID on the screen. It came across Private. It didn't dawn on me until I heard the clicking noise that it was probably the person I'd called earlier.

I wish they hadn't blocked their number when they called and I would have known for sure. My contact who knew about hacking wouldn't be able to trace the private call. Besides, more than likely, since I was using a TracFone, the other caller was probably also using a TracFone. They were untraceable.

Unbeknownst to Mom, I had a trunk of TracFones because some of my clients required the use of them. I was their accountant and their contact when they needed new phones. I lived a legitimate life but dealt with people who did some illegitimate things.

I needed to be getting some sleep because tomorrow I had back-to-back funerals. I loved working with numbers...but people, not so much.

CHAPTER 30

Omar

I loved watching Charity when she slept. There was still an innocence about her that I hadn't found in other women I'd come to know over the years. She put on airs that she was hard-core, but I realized that underneath that exterior was a kind and sweet person.

She was talented in so many ways. I was fortunate to have her as a part of my life. For the first time, I felt like I could truly be happy. My childhood wasn't the happiest. My mother did the best she could for me. My father was in and out of my life. Our relationship had been rocky.

My parents were never married. My father was considered a rolling stone. I'd heard he had other children out there. I didn't know any of them so as far as I was concerned, I was an only child.

Charity and her siblings didn't always get along, but I noticed that in spite of their differences, they loved each other and came together during the times of a crisis. I wished I had that.

Charity stirred under my arms. I squeezed her tighter. I got a whiff of her hair. She always smelled like strawberries—delicious.

I closed my eyes. My phone rang. I tried to answer it before it woke Charity.

"Hello," I said.

The voice on the other end said, "I need to see you."

"Now is not a good time."

"I'm outside."

"I have company," I whispered. "Charity is here. So now is not a good time."

"When will be a good time?" the voice asked.

"I'll come by sometime tomorrow. I'll call you."

"Don't make it too late. We really need to talk."

The caller hung up.

Charity said, "Omar, don't tell me that you have to go."

I placed my phone back on my nightstand and got back under the covers. "No, dear. It's something that can wait until tomorrow. Go back to sleep."

We cuddled. She fell back to sleep. I closed my eyes, but sleep passed me by. That phone call kept me woke all night long.

The next morning, Charity treated me to a home-cooked breakfast. Although I didn't have much in my refrigerator, she was able to fix two omelets.

"You can make magic out of nothing," I said as I ate.

"At least you had some eggs," she said. "Otherwise, you, my dear, would have been buying us breakfast."

After we ate, I walked Charity to her car. "I'll stop by later. Not sure of exactly what time, but I'll call you."

"Tonight, I have a dinner party," she stated.

"All night?"

"No, but I'm not sure of when I'll be home."

I leaned down and kissed her on the lips before closing her door.

I met up with my partner. We discussed a few cases. I created an excuse to work solo. I left the police station on a mission to find the person who had stopped by my place the night before.

While at the light, Slim's black customized Lincoln pulled up next to my SUV. He rolled down the passenger window. "What it do?" Slim asked.

"Taking care of business," I responded.

The light changed green. A horn blew from a car behind us.

"Make sure you do that," Slim voiced, before letting his window back up.

I continued toward my destination. After running into Charity at the hotel last week, I surveyed my surroundings more closely before entering. Ten minutes later, I was using the key I had and then entered.

I followed the man to the living room area of the suite and sat down on the couch. The television was on, but the volume was all the way down. I picked up the remote and increased the volume. I wasn't interested in watching comedy reruns. I turned the channel to a twenty-four-hour news channel.

"So you went against my advice? You're still messing with that Jones girl," Dad said. He drank out of a bottle he had in a brown paper bag.

"Dad, just because you have a problem with the Joneses, doesn't mean I have to," I responded. I threw the remote on the coffee table in front of me.

He sat down on the opposite end of the couch. "You're playing with fire. Are you seriously willing to risk everything to be with that woman?"

"Dad, my relationship with Charity doesn't affect you." His attitude about Charity really annoyed me.

"Omar, that's where you're wrong. You being involved with her isn't good for you. You're so busy with her that you're neglecting some things. Leaving it up to me to clean up the mess." He lit a cigarette.

"Charity is nothing like her mother. She's caring and sensitive. And she can also be a spoiled brat. I know the Joneses, or have you forgotten that?"

"She's nothing like you described. I don't know this selfish woman you keep describing to me. She's never been that way with me," I responded. He had me feeling like a teenager versus the grown man that I was.

He'd always had this effect on me. I found myself always trying to do things to please him. As a child growing up, I thought if I got his approval, he wouldn't leave me alone with Mom. He would stay and be around like some of my friends' fathers. But nothing I did back then made him stay, so why was I so concerned on pleasing him now?

"The Joneses are good at getting what they wanted. I've lived in their shadows for years. Trust me; I know."

"But Dad, you can't keep holding on to this vendetta you have against them. At some point, you will need to let it go."

"I'm letting it go. That's why I implemented my little plan."

"Because of you, an innocent man is in jail," I said.

"Isn't that poetic justice!" He laughed, but I didn't.

CHAPTER 31

Lexi

My kids were right. I was drinking a little too much. Drinking helped me forget about my problems and it helped me go to sleep. If I didn't watch myself, I could end up an alcoholic so I needed to make a conscious effort to cut back my consumption of alcohol. I laughed out loud. I used to complain to Royce that he was drinking too much and now look at me.

I walked to the sink and poured the entire bottle of vodka down the drain. I tossed the bottle in the recycling bin. I would no longer drown out my sorrows with liquor. I'd been preaching to my kids about the importance of prayer and living by faith all of their lives. Right now I was being a hypocrite; instead of practicing what I preached, I was not living by faith.

I'd prayed and prayed to God to deliver Royce from his situation, so instead of drowning in sorrow, I needed to act like it would happen.

Too much consumption of alcohol will cloud one's judgment. I'd been in a downward spiral of depression. I was stronger than that. I couldn't keep letting the circumstances beat me. Every now and then, you have to give yourself a pep talk and this was one of those times. Royce needed me. My kids needed me. I kept telling myself things to help change my mindset.

In spite of the police not doing anything to help Royce, I was not giving up hope. I called Lovie on his cell phone. He had already left the house before I got up.

"Mom, how are you?" he asked from the other end of the phone.

"Better. Much better. I hate you saw me like that," I confessed.

"You're stressed. I understand."

"No excuse. I'm your mother and a child should never see his mom like that. And I can promise you, that you never will again."

I could hear others talking in the background. "Mom, I have to run. Somebody forgot to bring the programs," Lovie said.

"Dear, where are you? I can swing by the funeral home and bring them to you."

"I'm at Lakeshore Baptist. But I have to leave here and go to Cedar Grove to this other funeral."

"You go do that. I'll swing by and pick up the programs real quick and drop them off at Lakeshore Baptist for you."

"Thanks. Nobody's answering the phone at the office."

"Don't stress. Mama's got this."

I grabbed my keys and switched into work mode. I shouldn't have had Lovie handle things by himself. I should have been helping out all along. I was too caught up in my own emotions.

The funeral had already started by the time I dropped the programs off, but at least they had them. I got back in my car and drove back to the funeral home.

Lovie was pulling up in the parking lot at the same time.

Once we were in Royce's office, I said to Lovie, "Son, you're doing a great job with taking over the business. Your dad would be proud. I owe you another apology."

"For what?"

"For not being here. I know how this operation runs. I helped set up the process. I should have been here with you."

"Mom, you're dealing with a lot. I didn't expect you to. I've got this. You just make sure you're all right."

My eyes watered. "My baby's not a baby anymore." I hugged him and kissed him on the cheek.

"Mom, don't do that."

"What?" I said, trying to sound innocent.

"Let's leave the mushy stuff for outside of the office." Lovie grinned.

He knew he liked it when I showed him affection.

I took a seat in the chair across from the desk. "So what's our plan for today?"

"I have two more funerals," he said while he looked at something on the computer. "I want you to stay out of trouble."

"Can you try that number back?" I asked.

Lovie pulled out the phone and called the number I'd gotten out of Diana's phone. He placed the call on speaker.

"Hello," a male voice answered.

"Hello," I repeated.

"Who is this?" he asked.

"I got your number from Diana. She said you could help me with something."

The caller hung up.

"Mom, maybe you shouldn't have said that," Lovie said.

"That should shake things up a little. You handle your business and let me take care of Ms. Diana."

I waited for Lovie to leave. I went behind the desk and retrieved the TracFone from the drawer. I placed it in my purse and left.

I needed to relax my mind so instead of getting a drink, I headed straight to the spa.

Two hours later, I was relaxed from a full body massage. My cell phone was ringing as I was walking inside of my house. I fumbled through my purse for it while deactivating the house alarm at the same time.

"Hello," I said, without bothering to look at the caller ID.

"Mom, where are you? You sound out of breath," Lovie said.

"I am. Trying to do too many things at the same time."

"Did you take that phone?" he asked.

"Guilty as charged," I responded.

"Fine. I wanted to make sure I didn't misplace it somewhere else. I meant to take it with me."

"I have it. In fact, I'm about to use it now. I'm going to call Diana and check on her."

"I should be home soon," Lovie informed me.

I hung up with him and went to my bedroom. I laid my purse and keys on the dresser. I removed the TracFone from my purse and dialed Diana's number. She answered on the first ring.

"Hello," she said.

"Diana, it's me, Lexi. How are you?" I asked.

"Now is not a good time," she responded.

"I just wanted to—"

"Nooo!" Diana yelled. Then the phone went silent.

CHAPTER 32

Royce

I needed to see Lexi in person. I didn't care if they were listening to our conversation. Mitch promised me he would give her the letter I wrote. Mitch said he would also try to get us a one-on-one meeting again but for me not to count on it.

My heart was heavy. I couldn't stop thinking about the young man who was killed because he was trying to help me. All of this waiting was getting to me.

I stood in line to use the phone. I dialed the house number. Lexi answered. I usually had my back toward the dorm, but not today. I turned my back toward the pay phone.

"Did you get the letter from Mitch?" I asked.

"Yes. I'm sorry to hear about the young man," she said.

"Me too. I was so close to finding out more."

"Royce, I'm concerned about your safety. I talked to Mitch about getting you moved. He said unfortunately, there wasn't anything he could do. If they moved you, they would put you in solitary confinement."

"At this point, I really don't care."

"Royce, is it that bad?" she asked.

I usually tried to sound chipper but not today. "Baby, I'm simply taking precautions. The death of the young man was a reminder to me I needed to stay on my Ps and Qs."

The recorder came on reminding us we only had fifteen seconds before the call would end.

"I'm going to call you right back," I said.

I hung up and called Lexi back.

"Do you remember Diana?" Lexi asked me.

The name wasn't ringing a bell. "I'm trying. Who is she?"

"Jason's secretary," Lexi reminded me.

"Did you try calling her back?" I asked.

"Yes, but her phone went straight to voicemail."

"Don't worry about Diana. She's not your problem," I said.

"She knows something. She sat there and told the police those lies and I'm not going to rest until she comes forth with the truth. And another thing, did you know she and Jason were having an affair?"

"That I'm not surprised about." Jason went through secretaries like other men changed underwear. I tried to tell him that he shouldn't sleep with his employees, but he didn't like to listen. I'd had to listen to many stories about his workplace issues resulting from his failed liaisons with some of the women he had gotten himself involved with.

"We found out Diana's been getting deposits from one of Jason's accounts."

"Since he's been dead?"

"Yes. So, we're trying to track it down to see who's been making these transfers."

A few men got in the line where I stood to use the phone.

"Babe, when the phone hangs up this time, I'll have to talk to you later. This line is getting long."

"I don't care. Let them get in another line."

"Babe, you know that's not fair. Besides, only one phone is working."

"What's not fair is the fact that you're in there and the real killer is roaming around free!"

"Lexi, calm down. I don't want you having a stroke while I'm here."

In a calmer voice, she said, "I'm sorry. I'm just so frustrated."

"You and me both."

The automated voice interrupted. "Babe, this phone is about to hang up. Love you and love the kids."

The call ended. I handed the receiver to the guy standing next in line. He made a smart comment. "Thought you weren't going to ever get off the phone."

I ignored him and went back toward my cell. One of the guards blocked the front of my cell.

"Jones, I've got a message for you," the pudgy guard said.

"From my lawyer?" I asked.

"No. From your son-in-law." The guard handed me an envelope. He moved from in front of my cell.

I held on to the envelope. I sat down on my bunk. I didn't have a son-in-law so I was curious to see whom the letter was from. I tore open the envelope and removed the sheet of paper inside.

The letter was from the detective dating Charity. It read:

Dear Mr. Jones,

I want you to know I'm doing everything I can to make sure you'll become a free man. Charity loves you and since I plan on becoming her husband one day, I must do everything I can to keep a smile on her face. Seeing you free will make her smile.

I am writing you because, although we don't know each other well, I thought out of respect I would ask you for your permission to ask her to marry me. You're probably thinking we haven't known each other long enough or well enough for our relationship to be taken to that level.

I beg to differ. I knew the moment I met Charity I wanted her to be my wife. Any man would be lucky to have her as his wife. I love her. I promise to take care of her. I promise to treat her just as well as you have.

I'm enclosing my phone number, 318-555-1212. You can call me collect at any time. It's my hope that by the time we get married, you will be a free man so you'll be able to walk Charity down the aisle and place her hand in mine.

Signed

Your Future Son-in-Law

Omar

I read the letter again. I gave him credit for approaching me on the subject, but didn't know if he was the best man to be giving my daughter to. I needed to know more about him.

I penned a letter asking for Omar to come visit me. After our visit, I would let him know whether or not he had my permission to marry my baby girl. In the meantime, I hoped Lexi would do as I asked and not concern herself with Diana. I didn't need to worry about her safety along with everything else.

CHAPTER 33

Charity

Mom insisted that Hope and I come over for dinner. I had plans with Omar so I didn't plan to be there too long. "Hope, you need to drive your own car. When we leave Mom's, I'm meeting Omar at his place," I said.

"Fine. I've got plans afterwards myself," she said as she grabbed her car keys from the table.

She beat me outside.

We followed each other to our parents' house. Surprisingly, Lovie wasn't there.

We exchanged hugs before taking our seats at the dining room table.

"Lovie's busy so he won't be here. Did he tell y'all he's moved in temporarily?" Mom said.

I looked at Hope. She looked at me. "No. This is the first I'm hearing of it."

"Well, I'm glad he's here. It's been lonely with your father not being here. What would make it perfect if you two decided to move back too," she said.

Hope beat me to it. "Don't mean to disappoint you, but we're all alpha females. I don't think we all could live under the same roof. Look at Charity and me. We get along, but there are days when she wants to be the boss and I want to rip her head off."

Mom said, "You're probably right. I'm being nostalgic right now. I keep reminiscing on when I had my entire family here."

I reached for her hand and squeezed it. "I miss those times as well. But we're all grown up now. Once Dad's home, you'll be glad we're not here."

Hope said, "Won't she? I remember walking in on them in the den. Ugh. Scarred me for life."

"Royce and I weren't that bad, were we?" Mom asked.

Hope and I said in unison, "Yes."

"Good. I'll be glad when he gets out so we can be bad together again." She paused and then said, "Your father knows how to be real bad."

"Mom, can we change the conversation?" Hope suggested.

I added, "Because we really don't want to hear anymore. I think we lived enough of it growing up in this house."

"I'll try to keep my thoughts to myself."

We ate our dinner. The conversation remained light until the end.

"I think something's happened to Diana. I tried reaching out to her, but her phone keeps going straight to voicemail. I've asked Lovie to check on it. That's why he's not here," Mom said.

"I hope she's okay. She's probably just not answering her phone."

"I also spoke with your father earlier today. He'd sent a letter by Mitch. Your father had been talking to a young man who knew that your father didn't kill Jason. Well, to make a long story short, the young man and the young man he was telling your father about were both killed."

Hope said, "This is becoming dangerous."

"Which means apparently we're on the right path," I said.

"I know we are," Mom said. "If I can speak with Diana again, I'm convinced I can make her talk. She knows a whole lot more than what she's been pretending to."

"Let's hope she calls you back," I stated.

Lovie walked in. "I'm afraid Diana won't be calling anyone back."

All of us looked in Lovie's direction. Lovie continued, "Diana's dead. She was found strangled in her room at her aunt's house. Her aunt is devastated."

"I need to call her aunt now and offer our condolences," Mom said.

She left the table and returned shortly holding the house phone. We could only hear her side of the conversation. "If there's anything we can do, let me know," Mom said.

She sat back at the table. "Whoever killed Diana wasn't a stranger to her. There was no forced entry to the home. The aunt had been visiting a sick relative. When she returned, she thought Diana was taking a nap. When she didn't come out for breakfast the next day, that's when she went to check on her and found her dead."

Lovie said, "I don't want any of you doing anything on your own. Mom, if you need to go somewhere, take one of us with you. Charity, don't be trying to play Nancy Drew and venture off on your own. Call one of us. Hope, I don't think I have to worry about you, or do I?"

"I'm too young to die. I'll tag along, but I'm not trying to do anything solo," Hope responded.

"Is that understood?" He looked at me and then our mother.

We both shrugged our shoulders. After listening to Lovie's lecture, I was ready to go.

My phone beeped. I looked up. "I have somewhere else to go so I will see y'all later."

I hugged Mom. "I'll call you tomorrow."

"Tell Omar I need to talk to him," Lovie said.

"About what?" I asked.

"Men stuff," he responded.

"Oh okay. Y'all got each other's number. Keep me out of it."

Thirty minutes later, I was parking in front of his apartment. I turned on the inside light so I could see how to reapply my lip gloss. Perfect.

I turned the light off and exited the car. I walked up the stairs. I noticed someone exiting Omar's apartment. I couldn't see his face for the baseball cap he wore. He walked past me without speaking. I stopped and watched him go down the stairs.

I knocked on Omar's door. "I thought I told you I was expecting company," Omar said as he opened the door.

"Who was that?" I asked.

"Nobody."

"You tell me that you answer the door sounding like you're mad and the person I just saw leaving your apartment is nobody. Come on now," I said with pouted lips.

He pulled me inside of the apartment. He looked outside first and then closed the door. "Forget him. I've missed you."

"I've missed you too, but—" I never finished my sentence. Omar pulled me into a tight embrace and ravished my lips with his mouth. I forgot all about the stranger.

CHAPTER 34

Hope

I felt guilty that I was about to embark on something enjoyable. Charity was at Omar's so she would certainly be out until the next day. I had asked Raymond to meet me at our house. I quickly changed into something sexy. Although I wasn't really ready for another relationship, I did want Raymond to find me attractive.

I removed the ponytail holder from my hair and allowed my hair to flow down to my shoulders. I sprayed on some oil sheen to give it a little shine. It was hot outside so I replaced my jeans with shorts. I replaced the tennis shoes with sandals with a small heel. I rubbed baby oil on my legs to give them a shine.

The doorbell rang. I checked my appearance in the mirror. I forgot to put on some lip gloss. I emptied the contents of my purse on my bed. The doorbell rang again.

"Bingo," I said as I located the tube I was searching for. I quickly put some on as I walked toward the front door. I placed the gloss in my pocket and opened the door.

"Hello, beautiful," Raymond said as he held out his hand and gave me a bouquet of flowers.

I took the flowers as he leaned down and kissed me on the cheek. "Come on in."

He followed me in. "This is nice."

"Thanks. Have a seat. I'll be right back. I need to put these in some water."

A few minutes later, I joined him in the living room on the couch.

Our conversation was filled with small talk and felt awkward at first. We soon got into a groove and the conversation flowed.

"Hope, you've changed a little."

I frowned. "Is that a good or a bad thing?"

"It's all good. You've always been this super-confident chick. But I'm beginning to see another side of you."

"Like I really have a personality. That I'm not some spoiled rich girl who thinks the world owes her something." I spoke very properly as I talked.

"Exactly. You sometimes came across like you were entitled to everything and that the rest of us were lucky to be in your presence."

I laughed. "Are you serious? Well, thank God I changed."

Little did he know the change was only recent. But at least my effort to change was working. If Raymond could see it, I hoped others would notice it too.

"When was the last time you talked to Maria?" Raymond asked as he looped his fingers with mine. He reached for my hand and kissed the back of it.

"It's been awhile."

"She told me you two weren't really talking. Maybe you should call her. She could really use a friend."

"You know what? Mom said the same thing. I might actually do that."

"I'm surprised you haven't convinced some poor rich man to marry you," Raymond teased.

"It will take a special man to tame me. I'm like a wild cat. Hard to tame."

"Don't let this nice guy complex fool you. I have some skills that can tame the wildest."

We were staring into each other's eyes. I forgot all about my rule of no men. We were thinking the same thing. I closed my eyes and our lips met. An electric current swept through my body the moment our lips touched.

Raymond pulled back first. "I'm sorry."

I bit my bottom lip. "I'm not."

"I'm sure you're used to guys coming on to you all of the time. I wanted to be different."

I grabbed his hand. "Raymond, you are different. Can I let you in on a little secret?"

"What?"

"I've always had a little crush on you."

"Why didn't you ever say anything?" he asked.

"Because you always had a lot of other girls around you. One thing about me hasn't changed is the fact that I do not like to share."

"If you were my girl, you wouldn't have had to share me."

By now my back was on the couch and Raymond was lingering over me. I placed my arm around his neck. "What about now? What if I was your woman? Would I have to share you?"

He planted kisses on my lips. "No. If you were my woman, you would have me all to yourself."

He leaned down to kiss me again. This time, I became the aggressor. I stuck my tongue down his throat. The passion that had been lying dormant for months reared back up.

The more he kissed me, the more I felt like my entire body was on fire. I eased out from under Raymond. I fanned myself. "As much as I want you right now, I can't," I said. "I promised myself I wouldn't do this."

"But... but we both want it," Raymond said.

I inhaled and exhaled. "You're right about that. I want you bad, but Raymond, although we went to high school together, we don't know each other. I want to know the Raymond of 'today,' not the Raymond of 'yesterday.'"

He sat straight. "You're right. We are moving a little fast. I apologize. I got caught up and, ooh, Hope. You don't know what you do to me. I haven't been able to get you off my mind since the night I saw you at Copeland's."

I sat on the couch beside him. "I haven't been able to stop thinking about you either. Which is weird for me because usually it's out of sight, out of mind."

"So where do we go from here?" Raymond asked.

I held his hand and led him to the front door. "You're going to think this is weird, but I've never been courted. I want to be courted. Do you think you can do that?" I placed my arms around his neck.

"I can handle it," Raymond assured me.

I gave him a quick peck on the lips. "Great. Goodnight, Raymond."

I moved. He wrapped his arm around my waist and pulled me back toward him. "Goodnight, Hope." He gave me a long sensuous kiss leaving me off-balance.

CHAPTER 35

Lovie

The puffiness under Dad's eyes made me concerned. I hadn't seen him since the meeting Mitch had scheduled. I picked up the black phone. I wiped it off and then placed it on my ear.

"Son, thanks for coming. How are you?" Dad asked.

It was hard seeing him behind bars. In spite of our differences in the past, my father had always been the best man I knew. He took care of his family and tried to instill in us good moral values. He'd always been, as far as I knew, a law-abiding citizen.

"I'm doing okay. Just busy."

"Nobody's giving you any problems, are they?" he asked.

"Not really. I have everything under control," I responded. Although sometimes I felt like I didn't. When some of my relatives wanted to cross the line with me, I would fall back and let them know my father was the majority owner of RJ Jones Funeral Home and as his son, that meant what I said went. I tried not to go there with folks, but sometimes they would make me.

"I heard from Mitch that your mother signed the papers. It's official. Lexi has control over all of my interests. If anyone gives you any trouble, tell her. She'll set them straight."

"Pops, I told you, I've got it." We both knew Mom would have done that, even without a power of attorney.

"What's been going on? I don't mean the sugarcoated version either," Dad said as he rubbed his head. "Keep in mind our conversation may be monitored."

That meant avoiding saying anything that could incriminate him or me but to still get my point across. I gave him the four-one-one on everything. "Mom thinks Diana knew more than she let on."

"Did the guy ever call you back?"

"No. I tried calling the number after we learned Diana had been killed and the number's now disconnected. We're sure all of this is tied up to Uncle Jason's murder."

"Sounds like it."

"I've told Mom, Charity and Hope not to venture off trying to do something on their own. Everyone we think may know something has ended up dead."

"Keep an eye on them, son. You know how stubborn they all can be; especially my Lexi. Once she gets an idea in her head, she's going to run with it and won't stop until she gets to the bottom of something."

I agreed. "Yes, that's Mom. She did promise she would make sure one of us was with her when she went on her fishing expeditions."

"Changing the subject, what do you think about this cat Charity's seeing?"

"Omar? As you know, I've never liked him. And that's because I recognize how whorish a lot of police officers are. Having worked at Bottom's Up, I've seen how scandalous some of them can be. I don't trust cops. Never have and never will."

"Well, he wants my permission to ask Charity to marry him."

"That's her business, but the verdict is still out on him as far as I'm concerned. Granted, he did help me out once."

"With what?" Dad asked.

During our conversation, I'd left out the fact that my apartment had been burglarized. "My place got broken into. That's another reason why I'm staying at the house."

"How much damage did they do?" Dad asked.

"They didn't take anything. They fumbled through my stuff. They were looking for something specifically and I have an idea of what it is."

"Is it in a safe place?" he asked.

"Yes. Also I'll be playing Robin Hood as soon as I leave here. Jason's ex-clients are going to be some happy people. Mom's going to be happy too because I found out Jason owed you more money than I'd originally figured."

"I could strangle him," Dad confessed.

"Too bad he's already dead," I said.

"Watch out for Charity. Watch that Omar for me."

"Pops, don't get me wrong, he's real good to Charity. I haven't seen him be disrespectful to her at all. Hope sort of feels like I do, but I think she's feeling that way because Charity's hardly ever around anymore."

"Your sister does like being the center of attention."

"Yes, she does."

Dad said, "I'll try to keep an open mind when it comes to Omar."

"You do that and I'll keep my eye on him for you out here. If he does one thing wrong, I'm going to tell Charity to dump him."

"Lovie, don't get into any fights. He's a police officer and if you fight him, he can easily have you arrested. There's no sense in both of us being in here."

"I'm not going to fight him. He'll wish he hadn't messed with a Jones."

Seemed like time went by fast. The guard said, "Jones, time's up."

"Son, I've got to go. Keep the faith. I'm not giving up yet."

That was good to hear. His eyes held a sparkle that wasn't there when he first sat down. Hopefully, my visit with him was encouraging. We said our goodbyes.

I noticed someone off in a corner staring at me as if he knew me. I stared back. I didn't know the dude. He tilted his head in my direction and then smiled before walking away.

I called Mitch as soon as I got in the car. "I just came from visiting my father and saw something he needs to know. Can you deliver a message to him?"

"Sure," Mitch responded.

"Tell him to watch his back."

"I'll be seeing him later this week," Mitch said.

"I need for you to see him today. This dude I saw made me feel real uncomfortable."

"I believe I can rearrange my schedule and make that happen," Mitch said.

"Thanks," I said. "Call me when you have." I needed to relieve some stress and I knew who I was going to call to help me do so.

CHAPTER 36

Omar

After having the letter delivered to Royce Jones, I used my credentials to set up a private meeting with him the following day. He seemed surprised to see me. I extended my hand out to him when he approached the table. We shook hands.

"How are you doing?" I asked as he took a seat across from me.

"I'm doing okay. I got your note."

"I meant what it said. I will do whatever it takes to make sure Charity is happy," I said.

"I'm going to hold you to it."

"You're probably not going to believe this, but for me, it was love at first sight. I knew the moment I saw her that I wanted her to be mine. To be my wife," I said.

"I felt the same way when I met her mother."

I grinned. "So you know how I feel?"

"Yes, Omar, I do. But my question to you is how does my daughter feel about you? Do you think she's ready for this type of commitment? She's been engaged before. Did she tell you about that?" he asked, looking me directly in the eyes.

"She cares about me. I can tell how she talks to me and from the things that she does. She mentioned this other guy, but she's never gone into detail. To be truthful, there's no need for her to. He was part of her past. I'm here right now and want to solidify our future."

"I can respect that," he said. "As long as Charity is happy, I'm happy."

"So does that mean you don't have a problem with me asking her to marry me?" I asked.

"Not going to go that far. I still don't see why you're rushing it. But on the flip side, I'm glad you're trying to make an honest woman out of her by doing the right thing."

"If you're concerned about me whoring around on her, that's not going to happen. I've had my share of tail. I want more out of life. I want love and stability. Charity's a beautiful woman and she can give me everything I need. There's no other woman out there that can replace her in my heart."

"You sound confident. I'm going to give you the benefit of the doubt. I might be locked up for now, but hopefully this is a temporary situation. But even if it isn't, if you hurt my daughter, you will have to deal with me."

"And that I don't plan on doing," I tried to assure him.

A guard came in. "Are y'all through in here?"

"Wrapping things up now," I responded.

"He thinks you're here asking me questions about my case. Lovie told me how you've been helping out. I appreciate that."

"I'll continue to do what I can to help," I said.

"I wouldn't want you jeopardizing your job, though. Be careful, young man."

"No, sir. I'm being real careful."

The guard came back. "Jones, you're the man today. You've got another visitor."

"Who?" I asked.

"His attorney. Jones, stay right here. We're allowing him in now."

The door on my side unlocked. Royce's attorney and I greeted each other.

I stood. "Mr. Jones, thanks for meeting with me."

Royce looked at me. "See you around. Take care of Charity for me."

"I will," I said, right before leaving him alone with his attorney. I slipped the guard a hundred-dollar bill before leaving.

My partner hit me up on the phone, chastising me for being missing in action. After I got Jake to calm down, I made a detour to the hotel to see my own dad.

He was lying across his bed in a drunken state. I hit his leg a few times to wake him.

He reached under his pillow.

"Dad, it's me!" I shouted.

"I thought you were a burglar," he slurred.

"Look at this mess. You've got clothes everywhere and you stink. Get up and get a bath."

He slowly got up. He stumbled when he tried to stand "Come on, let me help you."

I walked him to the bathroom. I turned the shower on and helped him into the tub. While he showered, I called room service and ordered some food. I started to clean up but that was what housekeeping was for. I made a mental note to call them later on my way out to clean the suite.

Dad walked out and plopped down on the couch. "Sorry you had to see me like that."

"I've been calling you and calling you. You had me worried for a minute," I said.

"I had to make an unexpected trip out of town."

Before I could ask any further questions, there was a knock on the door. I paid for the food and rolled the table inside. "You need to eat."

I watched him devour the food as if he hadn't eaten in days. "I'm glad you're showing so much concern," he said, in between bites.

"If I didn't care about you, Dad, I wouldn't be here. I wouldn't be helping you out like I have. I wouldn't be risking—"

He held his hand out. "I get the point. We don't have the ideal father-son relationship, but I do know you care for me. And I hope you know I care for you too."

"Yes. I only wish you would have shown it sooner."

"Son, I can't change the past."

I wished he could. I wished he'd been around more. Not just for when he wanted to screw my mother. I wished he'd been a better father to me before my mom passed. But I guess I should've been grateful that we did have some type of relationship now, strange or not.

"You saved me a phone call. What's going on with the Joneses?" he asked.

"There's nothing to report," I responded.

"I'm tired of playing cleanup."

"What do you mean by that?"

"Don't worry about it."

My cell phone vibrated. It was Charity. "Dad, I've got somewhere else I need to be. Lay low and please don't come to my apartment again."

"Don't put a woman before family, son," he said without looking up from his plate.

I left without any other words being exchanged.

CHAPTER 37

Lexi

I rarely left the house without full makeup. I'd forgotten to put on any lipstick. I walked and fumbled through my purse looking for a tube at the same time. "Oops, sorry," I said as I ran right into someone.

I looked and, to my surprise, it was Omar.

"Mrs. Jones," Omar said.

"What are you doing here?" I asked. I was in the lobby of this hotel and this was the last place I expected to see Omar.

"I'm here on a case," Omar said without looking me in the eyes.

"I'm meeting someone for dinner."

"I saw Mr. Jones today," Omar said.

"I didn't know he had a court date today." I reached in my purse for my cell phone.

"No. I went to Caddo Correctional Center to see him. I wanted to check on him for Charity."

"That's nice of you. I'm sure he appreciated your visit."

"Yes, we had a nice visit."

"Dear, I don't want to hold you up. I'm actually running late for my dinner date. Tell my daughter to call me, since I'm sure you'll be seeing her later."

"I'm actually on my way to see her now. This was my last stop."

I gave Omar a hug and went directly to the dining area of the hotel. I found who I was looking for and walked directly to the table. Mitch stood. "No, sit," I said. "Sorry I was running a little late."

Mitch replied, "No, problem. I just got here myself."

"I ran into my daughter's boyfriend."

"The detective?" Mitch asked.

"Yes. He claimed he was here working on a case, but I'm not sure about that."

"I ran into him earlier when I went to visit with Royce." Mitch pulled out an envelope from his pocket. "Royce wanted me to give this to you."

He handed me the envelope. I opened it and took a quick glance. I placed it back in the envelope and then stuffed it in my purse. "Royce knows exactly what to say to me to get me all mushy. He knows I don't like to be emotional." I grabbed the napkin on the table and blotted my eyes.

We were interrupted by a waiter who took our orders.

After the waiter left, Mitch said, "Royce is doing fine. The police haven't been successful yet in finding a weapon. They haven't been successful on much of anything, so hold tight. When we go to court, I should be able to prove reasonable doubt."

Mitch sounded convincing, but I wasn't going to rely on his legal skills to get Royce off. I wanted to provide hard-core evidence so there would be no doubt that Royce didn't kill Jason.

"Mitch, I'm going to be honest with you. I'm glad you're confident about things now. Before you were sounding like Royce was doomed, but I still will feel better if the police actually did what the taxpayers pay them to do. Investigate and find the real murderer. I can only imagine how many innocent men go to prison because of their negligence."

"Calm down, Lexi. When I look at things, I try to see all parties' views. I'm going to be honest with you. Royce had a lot of reasons for wanting Jason dead. Many people have killed for less."

"I know that. You know Royce. I know Royce. Royce works with dead bodies, but he would never kill anyone. We both know that."

"And you're right. Getting others to see that is my job and I promise you, I'm going to do my best to show that when this thing goes to trial."

"What about the video? Forget what Royce said. Use it. Lovie and I can deal with the aftermath."

"Royce is my client so I must honor his wishes," Mitch conceded.

"Fine. What if I had other information that could help you? Stuff that can show you that others may have wanted Jason dead. We've found out that quite a few of Jason's clients were unhappy. You want to know why?"

"I'm sure you'll tell me," Mitch responded.

"Because he was stealing money from them, too."

"We know that. But that hasn't resulted in any other arrests," Mitch said.

"Do you know that Jason's secretary was killed recently? She was found in her aunt's house strangled."

"No, this is the first time I've heard this. It could all be coincidental," Mitch said.

"Mitch, I don't believe in coincidences. Let's not forget Mr. Franklin was murdered, too."

"The police said it was carbon monoxide poisoning."

"Yes, by the hands of a murderer," I concluded. I didn't mention the inmate Royce told me about. I wanted Mitch to get an overview of what I knew so that maybe it would put some fire under him. "Mitch, what I wanted to meet you here tonight for was to plead with you to have the police reopen this case and find out who is behind this. Whoever killed Mr. Franklin and Diana is probably the same person who killed Jason."

"Lexi, right now you're speculating."

"That's more than what the police are doing. In fact, I'm doing their job. Where's my paycheck?" I threw my hand in the air. "There isn't one. So Mitch, I beg you to please talk to whoever you need to talk to because Royce can't go to prison behind all of this."

Mitch cleared his throat. "Royce is not going to prison. I will try to get them to do more investigating. I can't promise you anything."

I smiled. "All I'm asking is for you to try."

"Lexi Jones, you've been hiding from us," Mattie said. She was one of the Shreveport socialites whom I didn't like.

"No, Mattie, dear. I've just been busy." I didn't bother to stand. I plastered a fake smile on my face and looked at Mattie.

"We must do lunch soon. You haven't forgotten your husband, Royce, now have you?" Mattie asked, tilting her head toward Mitch.

No, this heifer didn't think I was stepping out on Royce with another man. I was sure she couldn't wait to get her gossiping tongue wagging.

"Mattie, this is Mitch. He is Royce's attorney."

Mattie's smile faded. "Oh, your attorney. I'm sorry. Hi, Mitch." They shook hands.

"Who did you think it was?" I asked as I batted my eyes.

"No one, dear. You go right ahead and finish your meeting. They're bringing your food now. I must go." Mattie rushed away.

I looked at Mitch. We both laughed. All I could do at that point was shake my head.

CHAPTER 38

Royce

Mitch delivered Lovie's message. Lovie didn't have to tell me to watch my back. I was on full alert. I didn't know who to trust in here so I trusted no one. The guards were making no effort to find out who had shanked the young man, either. They'd put us all on lockdown, but that ban had been lifted. Most of the inmates were now able to be in the common area to watch TV or play cards.

It was the end of another day for me. The lights were out. My cell door shut and locked. I lay on my back and stared at the ceiling, imagining the various marks were clouds.

I never thought I would miss seeing the outdoors. I would've done anything to be able to smell fresh flowers and to see a starlit night. If I was not in there and it rained, I would've stood in the midst of it and let the water fall all over my body.

I drifted off to sleep. I tossed and turned the entire night. I kept having nightmares that someone was trying to kill Lexi. That she was calling out my name. I could hear her, but the bars were separating us. I could see the masked man getting closer to her, but I was helpless. Right as he held his hand out to stab Lexi, I woke.

My body was drenched in sweat as if I'd really been doing the things that were in my dreams. I sat straight in the bed. I lay back down on the cot and turned on my side. This time I stared at the pictures of my family I had taped to the wall. I tried to remember when each picture was taken. I focused on the positive memories and drifted back off to sleep. This time I didn't dream or if I did dream, I didn't remember.

"Breakfast," one of the trustees said as he opened the cell door. He placed the tray inside of the cell.

I picked up the tray and brought it back to my bed. There was a piece of paper under the plate.

The note read: *Tell your family to back off or else.*

I almost dropped the plate. I looked out my cell and saw the trustee still in my area. He looked at me and walked back to my cell.

I asked, "Did you put this note on my tray?" I held up the piece of paper.

"Jones, I don't know what you're talking about," the trustee replied. "Let me see it."

"Never mind," I said.

"You must have been dreaming. Old man, get yourself together. You and I got ten more hours together. Don't want you spazzing out on me."

"I'm just stressed," I said. I slipped the paper in the pocket of the orange jumpsuit.

"You want a magazine or something? Something to read to take your mind off your situation," the trustee said.

"I'm cool," I responded.

"Eat up. That's probably the best meal you'll get today."

"Can I have another tray?"

"I'm not supposed to, but I'll get you one," the trustee responded.

Fifteen minutes later, the trustee returned with another breakfast tray.

I discarded the other plate and ate off the new tray.

I was going to stay in my cell the entire day but didn't want whoever to think I was scared. I was cautious but couldn't live my life in fear. Some of the young men spoke to me when I entered the common area. I held a magazine in my hand as if I was there to read, but I wasn't. If I wanted to read, I would have stayed in my cell where the noise wasn't as loud.

I found me a seat near the end. I pretended to be reading my magazine while scanning the area. I flipped the pages every now and then to keep up with the appearance that I was reading.

I noticed one young man watching me. I decided to test it out so I got up to get in line to use the phone. The young man whom I'd noticed watching me earlier did the same. He stood right behind me.

Sweat dripped from my forehead. I turned around and came face to face with him. We were pound for pound. His age was his only advantage. "You have a problem with me?"

"No, sir," he replied.

Some of the other inmates were looking in our direction.

"Then why are you watching me? Did I do something to you?"

"You look familiar."

I got closer to him. We could feel each other's breath. "Deliver this message to whoever you're working for: I don't take kindly to threats. If anyone, and I do mean anyone, in my family is harmed, I will see to it that they pay."

"But, I don't know what you're talking about," the young man declared.

"You know exactly what I'm talking about. I appreciate you giving me a little space." I moved my arms out.

The young man left and went to sit down. Since I was in the phone line, I decided to call Lexi. I didn't get an answer. I tried Lovie. He answered.

"Mitch gave me your message." I told Lovie about the note.

"Dad, I'm not going to let anything happen," he assured me.

"Son, I know you won't. I just wanted to warn you to be careful."

The call ended before I could tell him, "I love you."

The young man who'd been watching me earlier was no longer out in the common area. He'd returned to his cell and his door was opened. I stood in the doorway.

"If you or your people mess with me or my family, you will live to regret it," I whispered. "And I will make sure the people in here know you were the one that killed Jeremy." I spoke back in my regular tone. "Do we have an understanding?"

"Man, you don't…have to…worry about me," he stuttered.

"Good." I walked away and down the walkway to my cell.

I heard one of the inmates say, "Old man is gangsta."

I wanted to turn around and say, "No, not gangsta, but a man who's willing to do anything to protect his family."

CHAPTER 39

Charity

Omar greeted me at my front door holding a bouquet of long-stemmed red roses.

"These are beautiful," I said, as I took them and sniffed their fragrance.

Omar followed me inside. "Looks like you already have some flowers. Flowers that I didn't give you."

He was looking at the colorful floral arrangement sitting on the dining room table. "Raymond gave those to Hope. Aren't they pretty?"

"Whew. I thought I had some competition. Thought I was going have to step my game up."

"As long as you keep doing what you're doing, you'll be all right." I winked at him.

I placed the roses in a vase and placed them on the table next to the other flowers.

Omar scooped me into his arms. "You're ravishing. I could make love to you right here."

"What's stopping you?" I asked.

He kissed me on the lips and released me. "The night is just cranking up for us."

"Sounds interesting," I said as we held hands. I grabbed my small clutch and keys. I shouted, "Hope, I'm gone!"

Omar opened my door and I slid into the passenger seat of his sports car. We flirted with one another during the car ride to our destination. Omar pulled into the parking lot of a seafood restaurant known for its food and ambiance. It was located right on the lake.

We were led outside on the patio. To my surprise, the patio was decorated with beautiful orchids. The waiter held out my seat. "I'll be back with your drinks shortly."

"But I didn't order any drinks," I said.

"The gentleman has," the waiter stated as he held my chair.

I looked at Omar. He smiled. I took a seat.

Omar said, "Just enjoy."

The waiter returned with a bottle of wine. "This is a specially blended wine. It'll go good with your meal."

I looked at Omar. He tilted his head and mouthed the words "trust me."

I took a sip of the wine. "This is good. Sweet like I like my wine."

"I knew you would." Omar reached over the table and squeezed my hand.

Omar and I ate a meal fit for royalty. I sampled almost everything on the menu.

The waiter walked to the table and placed a covered plate in front of me. I held my hand out. "Oh, no. I can't eat anything else."

He looked at Omar. "The gentleman insists I serve you dessert."

"Omar, I'll have to get it to go. I'm stuffed."

Omar looked at me. "Please take a little bite."

"Fine. But if I burst, it's all your fault."

I removed the covering off the plate. My mouth flew open. On top of the plate wasn't a slice of cake or pie but a black velvet ring box.

Omar now stood next to me. He reached for the ring box and got down on one knee. He opened it. Staring back at me was a beautiful diamond ring with a sapphire band.

"Charity Jones, will you marry me?" Omar said.

My mouth flew open, but nothing came out. A marriage proposal was the last thing I was expecting.

Omar's phone rang.

"Shouldn't you get that?" I asked.

"I'm waiting on your answer," he said.

His phone rang again.

"It could be your partner, Jake. Maybe you should see who it is."

He looked at his phone this time. "I'll be right back."

I held the box containing the ring in my hand. I looked at Omar as he paced back and forth. I loved Omar, but did I love him enough to want to marry him? Things had been moving fast. He was very attentive to my needs. We'd only had one disagreement and that was because of what Hope had shared with me. Omar assured me he would be open and honest with me about everything.

He hadn't really given me a reason not to trust him. Being with him felt right. I deserved to be happy, right?

Omar walked up to me. I asked, "Do you have to go?"

"No. You're not getting off that easy. Maybe I didn't do this right."

He held his hand out. I grabbed it and stood. He wrapped his arms around my waist. "I love you, Charity. You complete me. You make me want to be a better man. You're my dream woman. You have my heart. I'm giving it to you to mold. I love you. You're entwined within my soul. So I'm asking you again, Charity Jones, will you marry me?"

I went with my emotions. "Yes. Yes, Omar, I'll marry you." How could I resist?

Omar kissed me in a way he never had before. I could feel his love transfer from his body to mine.

He removed the ring from the box and placed it on my finger. "I love you, baby." He kissed the back of my hand.

"I love you, too." I placed my hand on his cheek and stared into his eyes under the moonlit night.

CHAPTER 40

Hope

Raymond had awakened some feelings in me I thought were gone. I hadn't seen him since I'd asked him to come over the other night, but we'd been talking and texting on the phone. I didn't know if I would have the willpower not to give in to the lustful feelings I had. I really did want to make sure the next man I was with wanted me for more than my body.

I closed my eyes and let the hot water ease the sexual tension in my body. Twenty minutes later, I was sitting on my bed putting lotion on my legs.

"Hope!" Charity yelled out.

I jumped up and ran into the hallway. "What's wrong?"

Charity rushed toward me. She had her hand out. A diamond ring stared back at me. I looked at it and then into her face.

"I said yes," she said.

She waved her hand and jumped with excitement.

"You're getting married to Omar?" I had no issue curbing my enthusiasm.

"Yes. Let me tell you how he proposed. It was so romantic."

I followed her to her room. She sat near the head of the bed and I sat on the foot of the bed. I listened to her recant what had happened the previous night.

I smiled. "I'm happy for you," I said out loud, but in my mind, I wasn't too sure about things.

"Of course you're going to be my maid of honor. I've got to call Mom. Tell Lovie."

"For something like this, you better tell her in person. Don't call her on the phone," I said.

"You're right. Finish getting dressed. I want you to come with me."

I looked down. I wasn't wearing any pants. I went and got dressed and rode over to our parents' house with Charity.

We were barely in the door before Charity showed our mother the ring.

"Charity, this is beautiful. Omar does have good taste. I like the sapphire band. Different, but still classy," she said admiringly as she inspected the ring.

"We both agreed that we want a small wedding. Family and maybe a few friends," Charity blurted out.

"We can plan a wedding after your father comes home," Mom said.

"But he doesn't go to trial until later this year. I don't know if I want to wait that long," Charity said.

"What's the rush?" I asked. "Most people are engaged for months or years."

"We want to start our new life together as soon as possible. We love each other and don't feel like there's a need for a long engagement."

I looked at Mom and she turned away and looked at Charity. "You aren't pregnant, are you?" she asked Charity.

Charity stuttered, "I might be."

Mom dropped Charity's hand. "What do you mean? You might be. You know better than to have unprotected sex."

"Mom, it's not like he's some man I picked up at a club."

Why did Charity have to look at me when she said it? I no longer slept with men on the first date. In fact, I was trying to be celibate. Besides, this wasn't about me. This was about her and her fiancé, Omar. She needed to keep the attention on herself.

Mom remarked, "It's like this, Charity. I don't have an issue with you marrying Omar if that's the man you want to marry. But I do have an issue with you not taking the proper precautions to make sure you wouldn't get pregnant before you were ready. Being a mother isn't easy."

Charity shifted her body so that she was now facing her. "Mom, if I am pregnant, it might not have been planned, but I'm going to love this baby because it was conceived out of love. I think I will make a great mom. Don't you?"

Mom fell for it. She rubbed Charity's hand. "Yes, dear, I do. Well, congratulations to you both. I think."

"Yes, congratulations," I said.

Mom sent me to the drugstore to get a pregnancy test. She wanted to talk to Charity alone. I was happy to oblige them. For once, Charity was being the irresponsible one and not me.

An hour later, we were seated at the table eating breakfast, anxiously awaiting the pregnancy results.

The sound of the clock ticking seemed to intensify with each passing moment. "It's been enough time, don't you think?" I said. The suspense was killing me. I needed to know if I was going to be an aunt or not.

"I'll be right back," Charity said.

"Mom, if I told you I was pregnant, how would you react?" I asked.

"Like the time you thought you were but you weren't?" she responded.

I must have had a bewildered look on my face. Mom continued, "Yes, I knew about your little pregnancy scare when you were with Tyler."

"Who told you?" I asked.

"I'm Lexi Jones. Not too much gets past me."

"I can't take the suspense. I'm going to find Charity."

"Wait for me," Mom said.

We rushed to the bathroom located a few feet from the kitchen. Charity opened the door. "Well, it's official."

Charity was smiling so I still didn't know if she was pregnant or not. Why all the dramatics? She just needed to let us know.

"Spit it out already," I said.

"Fine. I'm not pregnant." She waved the stick in the air. It showed a negative sign. She threw it in the trashcan and then washed her hands.

Mom sighed with relief. I sighed with relief. Charity didn't seem too upset with the results, either.

"Now I can relax," Mom said. "Well, not truly relax, because now we've got to get your dad free so he can walk you down the aisle."

I listened to them talk about Charity's upcoming nuptials. I remained in the background fantasizing about Raymond.

CHAPTER 41

Lovie

Omar wanted me to meet him at this bar, but he was nowhere around. I sat at the bar nursing a glass of Cognac.

This used to be my father's and Uncle Jason's old hangout spot. Maybe one day I would settle down so I wouldn't be the old man in the club like some of these dudes who were still trying to mack on the ladies.

I laughed out loud while watching one guy who looked like he was a throwback from the seventies approach a female who looked to be around my age, in her late twenties. When she dissed him, he brushed his shoulder off and kept it moving to the next woman. Had to hand it to the old man, he was determined.

I felt a hand on my back and shoulder. "Lovie, sorry I'm late. Had to turn in this report before I called it quits for the day," Omar said as he took the vacant seat next to me.

"No problem. Gave me some time to relax my mind a little."

The bartender approached Omar. "What will you have?"

"Hennessy and Coke," Omar responded. "If I didn't have to get back to work, I would take it straight up." He laughed.

"I hear you. So what's going on? You got some news on my robbery?" I asked.

"No. That's dead in the water. I wanted to meet with you about Charity."

I stopped nursing my drink and shifted my body where I was now facing him. "What about Charity?"

"Well, Lovie, looks like we're going to be brothers. I asked Charity to be my wife and she accepted. Drink up. The next round is on me." Omar gripped his glass.

"Congratulations." I tapped his glass with mine. Although I was congratulating him, I was a little hurt. Charity should have been the one to tell me. I shouldn't have had to hear it from Omar. "When did this happen?"

"Last night. She wanted to tell you in person. I thought she would have by now. But when you didn't say anything, I decided to go ahead and let you know. Didn't want any secrets between us."

"I appreciate that, man. Charity's a good girl. She's a happy girl. Let's keep her that way."

"She's my heart. I don't plan on doing anything to hurt her. Like I told your old man, I'll die before I let anything happen to her."

"I'm going to hold you to it," I said as I turned back in my chair and motioned for the bartender to refill my drink.

Omar got a call from his partner and had to leave. I had two drinks but wasn't drunk so I left the bar and went to my parents' house.

Mom was sitting in the living room listening to some old school R&B when I walked in. She was nursing a drink of her own.

Mom looked at me, and then the near-empty glass. "I told you I wouldn't get drunk again. Never said I wouldn't drink anything."

"Mom, it's been a long day. I'm not going to judge you. I just left a meeting with Omar and had two drinks myself."

I moved past her and sat down on the chair.

"So you know about the engagement?" she asked. She took another drink.

"Yes. He couldn't wait to share the news. When did Charity tell you?" I leaned back in the chair and waited for her response.

"Your sisters stopped by this morning. We spent the majority of the day together so that's why I hadn't called you."

"I was busy anyway," I said. I sure could've used another drink, but reached into my pocket and pulled out some gum and chewed it instead.

"You're looking exactly like your daddy over in that chair," Mom said.

"I do look good, don't I?"

"Conceited like your daddy too." She laughed.

"I thought I got it from you."

"Him. Me. You are a Jones."

She stood and picked up her empty glass. "There's food in the kitchen if you want some. I'm kind of tired. I'm going to turn in early tonight."

"I'll find something. Go ahead and get you some rest." I dialed Charity's cell number. "I heard congratulations are in order."

"Lovie, I meant to call. I'm sorry. I was with Mom and when I got home, I fell asleep." I listened to her give me excuse after excuse.

"I was a little upset that I had to hear about it from someone else."

"I wasn't trying to keep it a secret," she assured me.

I replied, "You sound happy so that's all that matters to me."

CHAPTER 42

*O*mar

With Charity spending a lot of time at my place, I needed to rearrange my closet so she would have space for her clothes. My attempts to move a box located above the hangers resulted in it falling on the floor, spilling out its contents.

I bent down and placed the old pictures back inside. My eyes lingered on the last one. It was one of the few pictures I had with me, my mother and father in altogether. That was one of the happiest days of my life. I could remember it like it was yesterday. The picture was taken on my thirteenth birthday. My features were more like my mother's. Dad had admitted that he'd questioned whether or not he was my father until he'd gotten a blood test done proving to him that I was indeed his child.

My only regret was that no one outside of my family knew I was his son. I was his best-kept secret.

"Omar, are you in there?" I heard Charity ask.

"I'm in the closet. I'll be out in a minute." I placed the picture in the box and placed the shoebox near my other shoeboxes.

Charity opened the closet. "I saw both of your cars outside."

We greeted each other with a hug and kiss. "Moving some stuff around, in case you want to bring some of your clothes over here."

"We do need to talk about our living arrangements," she said.

My cell phone rang. It was Dad. When I didn't answer, he sent me a text.

"We can look for a place together," I said as I led her out of the closet.

We sat on my bed.

"Wherever we stay it must have a huge walk-in closet because Omar, you've seen my closet. I have a lot of clothes."

"You have enough to open up a store."

"Not that many," she replied.

"Yes. Charity, besides the women on TV, I've never ever seen a woman with as many clothes as you."

"Huge closet space is what I have to have. What's one thing you need for our new place?" she asked.

I lay on my side and looked into her eyes. "All I need is you. You're the only thing I need in our new place—wherever that may be."

I pulled her down on top of me. We kissed. I shifted our bodies until I was now on top. I devoured her mouth with mine. My phone vibrated, interrupting our flow.

"This better be good," I said to the person on the other end of the phone.

"I need you. One of the accounts I've been using to pay the hotel is overdrawn. How can that be when I had thousands of dollars in it?" Dad asked from the other end.

"I'm sort of busy right now. I'll take care of it tomorrow."

"Omar, I need you to do something for me," he stressed.

"I will. But it will have to be tomorrow," I said. I hit the *End* button on my phone.

"Who was that?" Charity asked.

"Jake," I lied. "He keeps bugging me about finishing this report. He's becoming a pain in my side."

Charity shifted. She was now off from under me. "Maybe you should take care of it. It sounded important."

"Are you sure?" I asked.

"Positive. Besides, I'm not going anywhere. You've got me for life." She held her hand in the air, showcasing her engagement ring.

I kissed her ring and then kissed her. "I don't have to leave to go anywhere. I need to access my computer."

"You do your work and I'll go fix us a little something to eat. Of course I stopped by the grocery store before coming over because you never have anything in your refrigerator."

"You're so good to me," I said.

"You know it." Charity blew me a kiss and left the room.

I got my laptop out of the bag and placed it on top of the bag. I went to my closet and returned holding a small notebook with login information. I went online and accessed one of my father's accounts so that I could transfer money.

There must be something wrong. The account had a zero balance. I accessed another one of his accounts and the balance showed zero. I wasn't sure of what was going on. I accessed several accounts and got the same thing. I was about to give up. I tried one more account. It still had money in it. I used the online banking and changed the password on the account. I wrote it down on the sheet of paper and made a mental note to tell my father his new information. I didn't have time to go in more depth because Charity was around.

"Nooo, it can't be!" I heard Charity yell.

I rushed out of the room and saw Charity passed out on the floor. My dad was hovering over her.

I pushed him out of the way and picked Charity up. "Charity, are you okay?"

She could barely open her eyes. "I saw him," she said before passing out again.

"I told you not to come here," I said to Dad as I placed Charity on the couch.

"You left me no choice. I need money and now." I rubbed Charity's hair off her face. I reached into my pocket and pulled out my wallet. "There's a thousand dollars in there. Take it. Get out."

"Son, I'm sorry. I didn't know you had company."

"Yes, you did. Now go before she wakes."

Dad took the money and left.

Charity woke and blinked her eyes. "I saw him. I saw a ghost."

"Saw who?" I asked, acting like I didn't know.

Her body shook in fear. She wrapped her arms around my neck and hugged me tight. "Uncle Jason. I saw Uncle Jason's ghost."

CHAPTER 43

Lexi

Ever since I had received the call from Charity the night before, I hadn't been able to sleep. I tried to assure her it was only stress.

She'd gotten engaged, thought she was pregnant and her father was locked up. Stress will have you hallucinating.

"Mom, what's wrong?" Lovie asked as he saw me pace back and forth in the kitchen in front of the stove.

"Have a seat." I fixed Lovie a plate while I talked. "Charity called me last night because she had a hallucination that she saw Jason. She passed out. Omar had to revive her."

"What do you mean? Is she in the hospital? Where is she?" Lovie asked question after question.

"She was at Omar's last night. She'll be going home today. I'm going by there as soon as I get you out of here."

"Mom, I could have stopped at Mickey D's or something. You didn't have to cook breakfast."

"Yes, I did. Cooking soothes me."

"Charity will be all right. She had a nightmare. Stop worrying."

"She wasn't sleeping. She was wide awake," I said.

"Stress. We've all been under a lot of it," Lovie said in between bites.

"You're right. I will feel better about things once I see that she's all right for myself."

After Lovie ate, I followed him outside of the house and got in my car and went straight to Charity and Hope's place. Charity was in her room changing clothes when I got there.

"Mom, I'm fine. I haven't been getting much sleep lately, so all of this is from exhaustion."

"Then get some sleep. Stop running behind Omar."

"He is not the problem," Charity said.

Hope stepped into the room. "Mom, you said you wanted to see me."

"Yes, dear. I was going to ask Hope to go with me, but after what happened, I will need for you to go instead."

"I'll be ready in about five minutes. I need to find my house keys."

"If you keep them on the table by the front door, then you will know where they are," Charity said.

Hope threw her hand up. "Whatever. Mom, I'll meet you at the door in about five."

"Take it easy. If you're stressing out like this now, wait until you get into the planning stages of your wedding."

"Mom, I'm an event planner. Planning stuff doesn't stress me out."

"Fine. I'm out of here. If you have any more hallucinations, call me immediately."

"I'm fine. Now go do what you were going to do."

Charity practically pushed me out of her room. Hope was waiting for me near the front door.

While in the car, I shared with Hope where we were going. "I promised Lovie I wouldn't venture out on my own. We're going to talk to one of Jason's neighbors. The one who claimed to have heard the noises the night Jason died."

"But you've gone over there before. You've left notes. But nobody's ever there or won't come to the door," Hope stressed.

"Until last night. I got a call last night to come by. I wanted to go first thing this morning before they changed their mind. They wanted me to come when the majority of the people on the street are at work."

I was told to park my car in the back in the alley and use the gate. I did as instructed. Hope and I walked through the backyard to the rear door. "This grass is messing up my white shoes," Hope said.

"I'll buy you another pair. Now stop complaining," I remarked.

I knocked on the door. The middle-aged woman holding a baby peeked out the curtain. I heard a few clicks.

"Come in. Quick," she said.

She opened the door. Hope and I walked in. We were barely in when we heard her slam the door. We followed the woman down her hall and into a room that had a table and a few chairs. The windows not only had curtains, but sheets were up.

"After what happened to Mr. Franklin, I've been like a recluse. I don't want what happened to him to happen to me. My husband's at work. I used to work in my yard, but now I'm afraid to."

"Lily, I appreciate you talking to us," I said. "You remember Hope? My youngest daughter."

"I sure do. This one here is my grandbaby."

I wanted to get past the small talk and down to what she had seen, but I knew if I rushed things, she might clam up on me so I went along with it.

"Well, Charles doesn't know I'm talking to you. He's told me to keep my mouth shut, but if that was my husband in jail, I would want someone to tell me."

"Lily, I promise you that whatever you say, no one will know you told me." I looked at Hope. "And Hope's not going to say anything, either. Isn't that right, dear?"

"Yes, ma'am. My lips are sealed."

Lily got up with the sleeping baby and went to another room. She returned empty-handed and took a seat. "The night Jason died, I saw you when you came by. I remember because Charles worked late and every time I heard a car door, I kept getting up to look. Well, before you guys got there, I heard something in the back. I looked through the window and saw two guys dressed in black go through Jason's back door. They were carrying a body."

"That doesn't make sense," I said.

"It doesn't to me, either. I saw Jason open the door and let them in."

"Why didn't you tell the police this?" I asked.

"Because I was afraid to. I talked it over with my husband and he told me I should stay out of it."

"But you told the police you saw my father's car out there earlier. You could have kept that to yourself too."

"After Mr. Franklin told them that, I decided to share it with them."

"But what you said led to my father getting arrested for something he didn't do," Hope said.

"Dear, Lily was scared too. Don't be mad at her."

"Lexi, I'm so sorry. I should have said something. But you have to understand. I'm all my grandbaby has. My daughter and her husband were killed in a car accident. Anything happens to me, I don't know what'll happen to my little munchkin."

"I understand. I'm grateful that you said something to me now. And I promise you we won't let anyone else know."

We left Lily to her own thoughts and guilt.

Hope was still shaken about what we'd learned. I squeezed her hand while keeping my other hand on the steering wheel. "Lily's explanation correlates to the video footage we saw."

"Yes, but it still doesn't help us figure out who did it," Hope said.

"We're getting close," I said. "I can feel it."

CHAPTER 44

Royce

I smiled, seeing my woman strut her stuff. She walked into the booth with her head held high. She took a seat. Our hands touched the glass. She blew me a kiss. I blew her one back.

"Girl, if I was out there, you would be in some trouble," I said to her.

She leaned forward so I could see her cleavage.

"You better stop that because you know it's hard to control the beast," I said.

Lexi laughed. I loved hearing her laugh. Hadn't heard it since I'd been locked up. "I've always loved that smile of yours," Lexi said.

"You've always known how to put a smile on my face," I acknowledged.

"Our little girl is engaged," Lexi said.

"I was going have to let her go some time or another. What do you think about Omar?"

"He's all right. He seems to be there when she needs him, and I can tell he cares about her."

"Good. After the last one she was with—and I'm not talking about Tyler; I'm talking about the jerk who left her at the altar—I don't want to see her hurt like that again."

"I don't think we have to worry about Omar. If nothing else, he's real attentive to her. The only complaint I know she has, and that's per Hope, is that Omar likes to monopolize a lot of her time."

"Well, that's not always a good thing, either. But like I told him and Lovie, as long as Charity's happy, I'm happy," I confirmed.

"Charity's agreed to wait until you're home before getting married."

"I don't want her putting her life on hold for me. If she wants to get married soon, let her."

"But, she wants her dad to walk her down the aisle."

"Fine, but if I don't get out of this, she can have Lovie walk her down the aisle. I don't want her or any of you putting your lives on hold for me."

"What are you saying, Royce?" Lexi asked.

"If something happens to me, I want you to find someone else." I didn't mean it in my heart, but felt it was the right thing to say.

"Royce Jones, stop talking nonsense."

"I'm trying to be realistic. Things aren't looking good."

"I have something to tell you that might change your situation. You can't give up yet," Lexi said.

"I'm not giving up. I'm trying to see things for what they are."

Lexi stood up to adjust her clothes and then sat back down. She whispered. I had to strain to hear. "His neighbor saw men bring a body into the house."

"Can you repeat that?" I asked.

"There were men carrying a body in the house."

"You need to tell Mitch this. Baby, with this new information, they have to let me out of here."

"They never saw any faces. With her lying at first, who's to say they will believe her this time."

Lexi had a point. What good was knowing the information if I was unable to use it? I clenched my fist. I was so frustrated I wanted to punch something.

"Look at me," Lexi said.

I looked at her.

"I love you," she said.

"I love you too." I shook my head. "I don't know how much more of this I can take. We get pieces of information, but not enough."

"I realize that it looks that way, but baby, I promise you, I'm going to put this entire puzzle together and when I do, you're walking out of here a free man."

I wanted to believe Lexi, but all of this was out of her hands. I'd prayed and prayed and only God could save me.

We spent the rest of the visit laughing and talking about old times. Some of the good times. One thing I'd learned while being behind bars was to never lose sight of the good times. I'd taken so much for granted. If God saved me from this situation, I would not be taking anything else for granted; especially my freedom.

"Jones. Time's up," the guard said.

"Looks like we never have enough time," Lexi said.

I agreed. "Until next time. Love you, baby." I kissed my hand and touched the window.

"Love you too, Royce."

I waited for Lexi to leave out first. Loneliness crept into my heart the moment I saw her walk out the door. I got up and walked out of the booth. It was a long walk back to my empty cell.

CHAPTER 45

Charity

I thought meeting up with my best friend, Lisa, would help take my mind off everything. She was late, as usual. I took the liberty of ordering a few of her favorite appetizers.

I heard her before I saw her. "My long-lost friend has decided to come up for air," Lisa said before taking a seat.

I held my head down in shame. "I'm sorry."

"I used to complain about you not getting out and dating. You went from a drought to never being available." Lisa removed her shades and placed them on top of her head.

"Lisa, I've been busy."

"That's an understatement." Lisa pulled out her cell phone. She stood. "First, give me a hug. And then let's do a selfie since I don't know when I'll ever see you again."

I hugged her, but then looked at her sideways.

"Smile," she said as she held her cell phone.

I did as instructed. She played with her phone while taking a seat.

"Lisa, I've been sort of M.I.A. these past few months, but I've been going through a lot."

Lisa lifted her hand. "Hold up. Stop the presses. Is that what I think it is?"

She reached across the table and grabbed my hand.

"That's one of the reasons why I called you to meet me here. I wanted to share my good news with you."

Her hand flew to her mouth. "Oh my God. When did this happen?"

"It happened a few days ago."

"And you're just telling me about it. Charity, you haven't been a good friend to me lately. But tell me details and I might forgive you."

Lisa was right. I'd been self-absorbed in my own world. I hadn't been talking to her or any of our other friends. If it wasn't business-related, I didn't make time to talk to others outside of my family and Omar.

"Omar's everything I've ever wanted in a man."

"I'm sure. But you know you have to watch out for these police officers. Some of them can be the biggest whores."

"Omar's not like that. He said he's been through his whore phase. He's at a stage of his life where he wants to settle down. Get married and start a family."

"So what do you need me to do? I can help you plan it. You know I'll have to throw the bomb bachelorette party. Whatever it is, I've got you," Lisa said. She seemed excited about my upcoming nuptials.

"I'm glad you're excited for me; some of my family members think I'm moving too fast."

"Nonsense. If you know he's the man you want to marry, why wait forever? All I need to know is do you want a big or small wedding and have you set a date?"

"We haven't set a date yet. And to answer your first question, we want something small. Hope's going to be my maid of honor and I wanted you to be my one and only bridesmaid."

Lisa frowned. "That's it. That's your wedding party?"

"Yes. I told you I wanted it to be small. Omar doesn't have a lot of family around so I wanted to keep it small and intimate."

"What about his parents? Will they be there?" Lisa asked.

The waiter brought out the appetizers. We filled our plates while we talked.

"His parents are dead," I responded.

"Sorry to hear that. What about your dad? What's going on with his situation?" Lisa asked.

"The police aren't doing their job. If they were, my father wouldn't be in jail now."

"I never thought he killed him. What are his lawyers doing?"

"His lawyer is building a case to show that it couldn't have been him, but in the meantime, we're holding our own investigation," I said.

Lisa stopped eating and gave me her full attention. "Do tell."

I gave Lisa a condensed version of what had been going on. "So as you can see, we're not leaving anything to chance."

"You can count me in as a character witness. Daddy Royce is like my second father. Although I don't blame him for wanting Uncle Jason killed, I knew he could never do it."

We chatted and got caught up with her life. The waiter brought the bill. Lisa reached into her purse. I stopped her. "I've got this. It's my fault we haven't been getting together."

"And I'm going to let you too." Lisa pushed her chair away from the table. "I need to go to the ladies room. I'll meet you in the lobby."

I paid for our lunch that was filled with appetizers and went to wait for Lisa in the hotel lobby.

I saw Lisa run in my direction. She said, "You'll never believe what happened." She sounded out of breath. "I saw a man who looked exactly like your Uncle Jason get on the elevator."

"What?" I said. "That's impossible." Then my mind recalled what had occurred the other night at Omar's.

I followed her to the elevator. We watched the dial on the elevator. It stopped on the seventh floor. I walked away with Lisa right behind me. I walked straight to the front desk.

The hotel clerk was on the phone. I wouldn't have interrupted her, but it sounded more personal than business. I cleared my throat several times. "Excuse me. I need some help here," I said.

"Let me call you back," the front desk clerk said to whomever she was on the phone with. She looked at me, and then at Lisa. "May I help you?"

I could not have cared less that she had an attitude. "Yes. I need to know if you have a Jason Milton staying at this hotel."

"And you are?" she asked.

"I'm Charity. I'm his niece."

Lisa and I watched her access their computer and appear to be looking for his name in their registry. She said, "I'm sorry. We don't have anyone listed under that name."

"Thank you," I said and walked away.

As we were walking out of the hotel, Lisa said, "They say we all have twins and I swear to you that man looked exactly like him."

"I believe you," I said. The question was why.

CHAPTER 46

Hope

I sat on the edge of Charity's bed and listened to her recount what had happened earlier at lunch.

"What did Mom say?" I asked.

"She thinks Lisa saw one of Jason's cousins. We're in Shreveport so that's possible."

"Then let it go. You're stressing yourself out over nothing," I stated.

The doorbell rang. "That's probably Omar. He's working late but wanted to stop by to see me for a minute."

We both left and went toward the front door. She greeted Omar with a kiss. I stood behind them.

"Hi, Omar."

He waved his hand. I shook my head. I went to the living room and turned on the television. I was bored. I was too young to be bored. But I was bored by choice because I could've been doing so many other things right then. I needed to find a balance. I was going from one extreme to the other. I used to be a party girl and now I couldn't remember the last time I'd gone out.

I called Raymond and he agreed to meet me at the new riverboat casino. I bypassed the two lovebirds and went to my room to get dressed. I put on a form-fitting black dress and three-inch heels. I complemented my outfit with a diamond necklace my parents had given me on my last birthday.

I went to tell Charity I was leaving but heard moans coming from her bedroom, so instead I sent her a quick text message.

For the next few hours, Raymond and I enjoyed each other's company. We ate at the casino buffet, then played a few of the slot machines. One of Raymond's frat brothers was performing in a band at the club located on the second floor of the casino so we spent the rest of our time there.

Raymond whispered in my ear. "I've really enjoyed myself."

The music was loud, but we were able to hear each other.

"I have too. I'm glad I called you."

"Would you like another drink?" he asked.

"Oh no. This one drink was enough for me. I still have to drive home and I'm not trying to get too tipsy."

"You could always come home with me," he said.

I smiled. "I don't think that's a good idea…yet."

He frowned. "You keep turning me down like this and you're going to flatten my ego."

I shifted in my seat. I placed my hand on top of his. "Raymond, I like you. I like you a lot, but as I told you before, I want to take things slow. See where things go."

"I've waited this long. I'm willing to wait longer," he replied. He bent down and kissed me on the cheek.

"I'm glad you understand."

A song from Rihanna's album *Good Girl Gone Bad* played. For me it was the opposite. I was a "Bad Girl Gone Good" and I liked it.

Raymond and I danced until after midnight. He escorted me to the front of the casino. I gave the valet my ticket for him to bring my car around.

"Raymond, I've had a great time."

"What are you doing this weekend? I hear Maxwell's supposed to be here performing."

"I would love to go."

"The concert is Saturday and starts at eight, so I'll come get you around seven," he said.

"Sounds good."

The valet drove up. I kissed him lightly on the lips. "Goodnight, Raymond."

I gave the valet a tip. He held my door open and I got inside of my car. Raymond waved at me. I waved back.

I drove away. I hopped on the interstate so I could bypass the majority of the lights on the way home. I didn't notice a car following me until I got off on the Lakeshore Drive exit. Whatever lane I got in, the car behind me did the same. When I stopped, they stopped. I decided to stop in the twenty-four-hour gas station. The parking lot was filled with other cars and people. The car behind me did the same.

I pretended to need some gas, but instead I kept driving and drove around the gas pumps and got back onto Lakeshore Drive.

The car behind me still followed.

I had my Bluetooth turned on in my car so while driving, I activated it and said, "Call Lovie."

Lovie answered. "Hope, do you know how late it is?"

"Someone's following me. What should I do?" I blurted out.

Lovie's tone changed from chastisement to concern. "Where are you?"

"On Lakeshore. Was going to take it all the way home."

"Drive straight to the police department. I'm on my way."

"But—"

"Don't argue with me. Whoever it is following you will get the message."

I did as instructed. I turned on one of the side streets and made a circle back on to Lakeshore Drive. I hit the interstate and got off on the exit that would take me straight to the police department.

I pulled into the parking lot. There were only a few cars in the lot, but the person who was following me kept on driving. I waited to see if they were going to turn around and come back; they never did.

A few minutes later, Lovie parked beside me. He got out of his car and came to my driver's side. "Are you all right?"

"No." My hands were shaking.

"We can leave your car here and come back and get it tomorrow," he said.

"I'm fine enough to drive myself home," I stuttered.

"What kind of car was it? Did you see a driver?" Lovie asked.

"It was either a black or dark-blue Caddie. The reason I know it was a Caddie was because of the grille in the front. I couldn't tell who was driving it. I did notice a baseball hat," I said. This time my words were clear.

"I'm going to follow you home," Lovie said.

He got no argument from me. If he hadn't suggested it, I would have insisted that he did.

CHAPTER 47

I decided to spend the night on my sisters' couch in case whoever was following her knew where she lived.

My phone ringing woke me.

"Lovie, it's seven in the morning; where are you?" Mom's voice rang from the other end.

Having to check in with her was the downfall of us now staying under the same roof. I decided not to upset her and tell her about what had happened with Hope last night.

"I had to get out and take care of something. Everything's fine."

"Next time, leave me a note or something. You up and disappeared."

"Mom, I'm a grown man. I don't need you lecturing me."

"I know that. I'm sorry, okay."

Mom had a good way of making you feel guilty about something you shouldn't feel guilty about. "Mom, no need to apologize. We're all under stress. I understand."

We ended our call. I went outside to check on our cars. I didn't notice last night, but I noticed this morning that Charity's car was missing. I went back inside and up the stairs to see if she was in her room.

Hope was sound asleep and Charity's door was open and empty.

I hated to wake Hope but I did. Thirty minutes later, she dragged herself into the living room. She had her hair pulled back in a ponytail and was wearing a pink jogging suit.

"Sis, I think you should pack a bag and come back to the house and stay with me and Mother. Charity's always gone with Omar and I don't think it's safe for you to be staying here by yourself."

"Lovie, don't let me regret calling you. Mom and me under the same roof? Nope. That's not going to happen. We're like oil and water. We are not going to mix."

"At least make sure you activate the security system. I was able to leave out and the thing didn't go off. No use of having one if you're not going to use it," I said.

"Fine, I'll make sure I keep it activated. I'll tell Charity to do the same whenever she comes home."

"I've got things to do so lock the door and activate the security system."

I hugged Hope and left her home alone. I dialed Charity's number. I didn't get an answer. I called Omar. He answered.

"Let me speak to my sister. Better yet, put it on speakerphone. That way I don't have to repeat myself."

"Charity's not here," Omar said.

"What do you mean, Charity's not there? Hope told me she was at your place."

"I haven't seen Charity since yesterday evening when I stopped by. I had a late-night surveillance but wanted to see her because it was going to be late when my partner and I finished."

I pulled over to the side of the street. "I've got to locate my sister. If you hear from her, tell her to call me or you call me."

I disconnected our call. I called Charity's number again. Nothing. The call went straight to voicemail. I called Hope. Hope didn't answer. I hit my steering wheel. I almost got hit when I pulled back onto the road without looking. The driver behind me honked his horn.

I sped down the street back to my sisters' house. I sighed with relief when I saw Charity's car. I slammed on my brakes, turned the car off and ran down the walkway to their front door.

Charity opened the front door. I hugged her so tight that I lifted her off the floor.

"Why aren't you answering your phone? You had me worried about you. You're trying to give me a heart attack and I'm not even thirty yet." I was frantic and out of breath.

"Lovie, calm down. I'm fine. I spent the night at Omar's, but he never came home so I got up early and came back here."

"You should have told somebody. If not me, at least Hope."

"I didn't know I needed a babysitter," she snapped.

"Call Omar. I got him looking for you too."

Hope came into the room. "Lovie, I got your message. I was in the bathroom. I was about to call you back when I heard you out here."

"She's here. You girls are going to be the death of me. Somebody needs to know where you are at all times." I looked at each one of them when I said it.

"Lovie, we're grown women. We don't have to check in with anyone," Charity proclaimed.

"Tell that to Mom after I tell her about what happened to Hope last night." I folded my arms.

Charity looked at Hope. "What is he talking about?"

Hope gave her a quick recap from last night.

"Why didn't one of you call me? I would have come home," Charity said.

"We don't have to check in with each other, remember," I said, in the most sarcastic tone I could think of.

My cell phone rang. It was Omar. I answered. "I found her. She's home. Yes, I'll tell her to call you."

After making sure both of my sisters were home safe and secure, I left to go to the funeral home. At least there, I didn't have to worry about any drama.

CHAPTER 48

I stood in the doorway waiting for Charity to come. I pulled her into my arms and held her tight.

"Babe, I'm all right. You can let me go now," Charity said.

I released her. She walked inside and I closed the door.

"I didn't realize you had been here until you told me. I'm a detective and couldn't tell someone had been in my house. Please don't tell Jake that," I teased her.

"I was trying to surprise you, but the surprise was on me," she said.

"I'm glad you're here now, though." We were now seated on the couch.

"We were supposed to go out, but I think I want to stay in. I don't feel like being around a lot of people," Charity said.

"I'll order a couple of pizzas and we can watch movies on Netflix," I said.

Over the next few hours, we ate, cuddled and watched movies. For once, there was peace in my life. Charity dozed off in my arms. I smiled because soon she would become Mrs. Underwood.

My cell phone rang. I tried to answer it before it could wake Charity. I didn't bother to look at the caller ID. "Hello."

I got off the sofa and walked to the other side of the room.

"Son, we need to talk."

I whispered, "Your timing is always off. I'm busy right now."

"You're with that Jones girl, aren't you?" Dad asked.

"Yes, so I really must go."

"You're playing with fire."

"Dad, I must go. I'll call you back later." I disconnected the call.

"Dad? I thought you told me your father was dead," Charity said.

I turned around. She was now sitting straight up on the sofa. "I thought you were sleep."

"Answer the question. Is your father dead or not?" she asked.

"It's complicated." I walked back to where she was and took a seat next to her.

Charity crossed her arms and leaned back on the sofa. "I'm listening."

"You really didn't hear what you thought you heard."

Charity tilted her head. "Omar, the worst thing you can do is lie to me. I know what I heard."

"I didn't ever say my father was dead. I told you my mother was dead."

"When I asked you if your parents were living, you told me they were dead. Please don't play games with me. I'm giving you one more chance to be honest with me." She blinked her eyes a few times.

"Yes, my mother is dead. My father is not. He's still around."

"Great. So when can I meet him?"

"I'm not sure if that's a good idea," I said. I couldn't have her meet my father. If I did, she definitely wouldn't want to marry me. I couldn't risk losing her because of him.

"Well, I think it is. Call him. Let's schedule a time. Tonight. Tomorrow. This weekend." Charity kept spouting out dates.

"I'm not going to call him. He's fine where he is. My dad and I don't actually get along. We're nothing like you and your dad."

"Regardless, if you and I are getting married, I need to meet him."

"Charity, drop it, okay? I don't want you to meet him. Isn't that good enough for you?"

"No. Not without a valid reason."

"He's not a good person."

"But he's still your father and I want to meet him."

"No. And I'm through discussing it," I snapped.

Charity jumped off the couch and grabbed her keys and purse. "Bye, Omar. Call me when you feel like continuing this discussion."

I stood and blocked the front door. "Charity, calm down. You're too upset to be driving anywhere."

"Move, Omar."

"No, not until you listen to me."

Charity tapped her foot. "Now you want to talk."

"I hate that my father isn't a good man. I don't want you to meet him and then change your mind about marrying me."

Charity reached for my hands and held it. "Omar, is that what you're worried about? Baby, I love you. So what if your father wasn't the best dad to you. He is not you. You're a good man. You've been good to me. You're always helping others. I wouldn't dare let who your father is stop me from loving you."

I felt a little more secure with her response. I moved from in front of the door. "Promise me, you'll stay. We can talk about this later. For now, let me love you."

She didn't resist when I kissed her. I scooped Charity in my arms and carried her to my bedroom and made love to her. She fell asleep in my arms. Sleep escaped me. I couldn't allow my past to intersect with my present. If Charity ever found out who my father was it would be the end of our relationship. It had taken a lifetime to find a woman like Charity and I would not lose her. I couldn't lose her. I didn't want my life to go back to the way it was before her.

I heard a knock at the door. I eased out of the bed. I opened the door but wouldn't allow the person on the other end inside.

"You are making me regret I agreed to help you," I said.

"Son, you are allowing a woman to get in between us," my father said from the other end.

"I never felt right helping you. I only did it because I thought you would finally give me your approval. That you would finally love me. But Dad, I don't think you're capable of loving anyone else but yourself."

"Omar, that's not true. I love you. I've loved you from the moment I laid eyes on you."

"You had a funny way of showing it. All of my friends' fathers attended their ball games. Me, I stopped playing ball and the gang became my family. The leader became my father figure because my own father wouldn't ever publicly acknowledge I was his son."

"I thought we'd discussed this. Thought you were clear on why things happened, but obviously not. Are you going to let me in or not?" he asked.

"Charity's in my bed. As I told you on the phone, now is not a good time."

"But, Omar, I need you."

"I needed you back then. Now you know how I feel." I shut the door.

CHAPTER 49

Lexi

I didn't want to alarm my children, but I'd been getting a lot of hang-up calls. The caller always called from a blocked number and they would sit and hold the phone until my voicemail disconnected the call.

The doorbell rang.

I wanted to cook dinner for the kids tonight but didn't have everything I needed. I didn't feel like going to the grocery store so I called and used a delivery service. I retrieved cash out of my purse and went to the front door.

"Ms. Jones?" the young deliveryman said. He was carrying several plastic bags.

"Come on in," I responded. "Put them right there."

He placed them on the table. He handed me the receipt. I double-checked to make sure everything on the receipt was in the bags. The grocery items were prepaid for. I handed him a twenty-dollar bill for his tip.

His eyes sparkled. "Thank you, Ms. Jones."

"You're welcome. Thanks for not taking all day to deliver."

"Do you want me to take them to the kitchen for you?"

"No, I've got it. Please close the door when you leave."

I gathered the handles of the plastic bags and took them to the kitchen.

I went upstairs to change into another outfit. I didn't want to get the pantsuit I had on dirty with food. On my way back downstairs, I noticed the front door wide open.

"Lovie, is that you?" I called out.

No response. I called out Charity's and Hope's names. Still no response. I ran back upstairs into my bedroom. I retrieved the gun from under Royce's pillow.

I called Lovie. "Someone's in the house."

"Lock your door. I'm calling the police," Lovie said frantically from the other end.

I ran to my bedroom door, shut it and locked it. Lovie placed me on hold while he made the phone call.

"The police are on their way. I'm on my way too," Lovie said. I could hear the beeping noise from his car as he started the engine.

"I've locked the door. I don't hear anything," I said.

I walked to the window and looked outside. I noticed a car near the end of the driveway parked near the street. "I see a dark-blue car. Looks like a Cadillac parked by the end of the driveway."

"That's the same car that followed Hope the other night."

"Why am I just now hearing about it?" I questioned.

"Didn't think it was relevant," Lovie responded.

I heard sirens. "The police are near. I hear them. Oh my goodness. There's a man running out the front through the yard."

"Do you recognize him?" Lovie asked.

"Not really. He's wearing all black and a baseball cap. He's getting into a Cadillac. He just pulled away."

The police car pulled behind my car seconds after the other car drove away.

"The cops are here," I said to Lovie.

"I'm almost there too," Lovie stated.

"I'm going to get off this phone and tell them they're a minute too late."

We ended our call. I greeted the two uniformed officers at the front door.

"We got here as soon as we received the call," the shorter police officer said.

I told them what happened. While talking to them, Lovie came in. They drew their guns.

"Relax. That's my son," I said. Whew, I said to myself. They were some trigger-happy police officers.

"And your name?" the shorter officer asked.

"I'm Lovie Jones. I'm the one who called you." Lovie took a seat next to me.

"Mrs. Jones, you say there's nothing missing. If you can think of anything else, please don't hesitate to call us."

The other officer handed me his card. I placed it on the table in front of me.

Lovie walked them out. I walked to the kitchen. I wasn't in the mood to cook anymore. Lovie remained silent as he helped me put up the groceries.

When we were through, I turned and faced him. "I think we're real close to finding out who killed Jason. Otherwise, the incident with Hope or with me wouldn't have happened. Can you check to see if anyone on the street has video footage outside of their homes?" I asked Lovie.

"I'm on it."

"I should have listened to Royce and gotten a better security system. If I had, I would know exactly who this mystery man was."

"Mom, one question," Lovie said.

"What?"

"Why wasn't the alarm set? You're here by yourself. I told you to keep the alarm activated. I swear y'all won't listen to me."

"Lovie, I forgot. I ordered groceries. I paid for them. I told the delivery boy to close the door." I paused." I never checked to make sure the door was locked. It's my own fault."

Lovie placed his arm around me. "Mom, you can't be careless. Too much stuff is going on."

"I know." My hand went up to my forehead. "Your dad called while I was talking to the police. I didn't accept his call. I didn't want him to worry. If he calls you, don't tell him what happened."

"I can't promise you that," Lovie said.

"You Jones men can be so stubborn."

"I get it from my mama," Lovie said.

I couldn't deny it. I could be stubborn. I don't like being scared. This incident today had terrified me. I should not have been scared in my own house.

CHAPTER 50

Royce

I listened as Lovie told me about the intruder at the house. My head started pounding. If I had been there, it wouldn't have happened. How many times had I told Lexi to set the alarm? Maybe now, she would start using it more frequently. Out of frustration, I hit the phone with my fist, not caring if I hurt it.

"Jones, one more outburst like that and you will be banned from using the phone," the guard on duty said.

I didn't want to lose my phone privileges, but it was either the phone or punch him, and if I hit the guard, I would be put into solitary confinement and brought up on additional charges.

"Lovie, offer the neighbors money or whatever you have to do, but find out who it was in the car."

"I'm on it. I'm waiting on Mr. Branson to get off work and he's going to show me his footage."

"I was wondering what was going on. Thanks for telling me. I'm sure your mom told you not to tell me."

"I don't want to lie," Lovie responded.

"You don't have to. I know her. This is the reason why I need to be out there. I should be there to protect my family."

"Even if you were out of jail, you would have been at the funeral home. So don't beat yourself up about it," Lovie said.

He was right. I was feeling helpless. I couldn't protect Lexi from in here. I couldn't protect any of them while locked in this place. "This call's about to end. Tell your mom I'll call her later. Love you."

The call disconnected. I dialed Mitch's number. He answered. After waiting on the automated recording, I said, "I don't care who you have to pay off, but I need you to get me out of here."

"Royce, calm down. You know I can't do anything like that."

"You've done it before."

"Royce, you do know these lines may be recorded."

"At this point, I don't care. I want my freedom. I've been more than patient. I didn't kill Jason. You know it and I'm sure the police know it as well. They don't want to admit they made a mistake."

"I'm working on it. But what I need for you to do is calm down. You're not going to do any of us any good if you go flying off at the mouth like this."

"That's the problem. I've been too quiet. Call the reporter from Channel Twelve. I'm ready to talk."

"Royce, as your legal counsel, I am going to advise against this. Let me handle it."

"Mitch, aren't I paying you?"

"Yes," he responded.

"Then do as I said. Schedule the interview. I have a few things I need to say."

"But, Royce," Mitch pled.

"Now… Set it up. I'll be waiting." I slammed the receiver down, almost breaking the phone.

The next morning after breakfast one of the guards informed me I had a visitor.

"It's in the main room. Not the regular visitation booth," the guard said.

I followed behind him. He opened the door. Seated were Mitch on the side of the table where I normally sat, and also inside were the reporter and cameraman from the local news station.

Renee Winger turned and faced me. "Mr. Jones, I wanted to thank you for agreeing to talk to me."

We shook hands. I took a seat next to Mitch. Mitch said, "Against my advice."

I cleared my throat. "Thank you for this opportunity to talk to your audience."

Renee said a few things to the cameraman and then sat down right across from me. "We don't have much time so we're going to get things rolling. Craig, are you ready?"

Craig, the cameraman, nodded.

"Mr. Jones. You're speaking with us against the advice of your attorney, is that correct?" she asked.

"Yes."

"Many were shocked, myself included, when we learned that you were the lead suspect in the murder of businessman Jason Milton."

"Lead? Apparently, I was the only suspect. The police arrested me under false pretenses while Jason's real killer runs free."

"So you're saying that you didn't kill Jason Milton?" she asked.

I looked directly in the camera. "No, I did not kill Jason and as long as I'm in jail, his real killer is out terrorizing my family. I wanted to do this interview today to send a message to this person. You may have gotten away with killing Jason, but if you harm my family, I will make sure I find out who you are and you will pay."

"Ladies and gentlemen, I wasn't expecting this. You don't think it's some of Jason's relatives trying to get some type of revenge, do you?" Renee asked.

"No, I don't. I think Jason's real killer feels that we know something. Something that can prove my innocence. I'm putting him on notice. We do. So whoever you are, I suggest you turn yourself in and admit what you did."

"Mr. Jones, I'm sorry, this is all the time we have. Thank you again for talking to me."

"My pleasure. I want to get out of here and get back to my life," I said.

The cameraman turned off the camera. Renee said, "Mr. Jones, for the record, I believe you're innocent. I am going to make some phone calls to the police department and see if I can convince them to reopen this case. I've talked to many people who were guilty of the crimes they committed and you're not one of them. I believe you're an innocent man."

"I am. Thank you," I said to her.

She and the cameraman left Mitch and me alone.

"Royce, I still don't think it was a good idea."

"I know you don't. I need you to give this note to Lexi." I handed him an envelope with Lexi's name on it. "And give this one to Lovie." I handed him another envelope. This one had Lovie's name on it. "Whoever killed Jason is going to turn it up a notch or two after they see my interview. I need for my family to be on high alert."

"I can hire some professionals to watch them if you like."

"Mitch, please don't take offense to what I'm about to say." I stared him straight in the eyes. "I've been depending on you and others the entire time I've been here. No more. Us Joneses got this. Just answer when I call." I got up and knocked on the door. "Guard, I'm ready."

I was no longer feeling defeated.

CHAPTER 51

Charity

I kept looking at my cell phone; hoping that Omar would call me back. We had another argument. I still wanted to meet his father. He insisted he didn't want me to. Now, I was at my parents' house listening to Lovie give us a lecture on being cautious.

Yada. Yada. Yada. Hurry it up already, I said to myself.

Mom said, "Lovie and I got a note from your dad. He's going to be on the news. Lovie, turn up the volume."

As if on cue, our dad appeared on the television screen. We watched the interview. "Dad seems real upset," Hope said.

"Duh," I snarled.

"So now that he's done the interview, whoever followed Hope and broke in here will probably do something else drastic. We want you to be conscious of your surroundings. Be sure to activate your house and car alarms. Do not leave any doors unlocked."

"Lovie, we've got it. We don't need you to repeat yourself," I said.

"And don't get too comfortable because you're dating a cop," Lovie said.

"I'm going to keep my normal routine. I'm not going to let someone change how I do things," I stated.

"Charity, you're stressed, but watch your tone with your brother. He's only concerned about your safety."

"Yes, Mom." I looked down at the floor.

"I swear it seems like the roles have reversed between you and

Hope. I expect this type of behavior from Hope, but you. You're usually the more sensible one."

Hope said, "Hey, keep my name out of her mess. What she's doing is all her."

I rolled my eyes at Hope. I looked back at Mom. "I'm having one of those days. Okay."

"Get over it. You need to regroup and focus. Forget the petty little stuff right now. Look at the bigger picture. Did you see the strength your father displayed in a few minutes in an interview?" she asked. "He hasn't given up so we're not, either."

The doorbell rang. Lovie went to the door. He returned holding a disc. "This will tell us who broke in."

Lovie went to the DVD player and placed the disc inside. He retrieved the remote control and pressed the *Play* button. The footage was fuzzy.

"I still can't see his face," Mom said.

"Me neither," Lovie said.

"Slow it down and then pause it," Mom said.

Lovie did as instructed. I got on the edge of my seat and looked at it closely. Although the face was fuzzy, the stance of the man and the hat looked familiar.

"Girls?" Mom asked.

"That's the car that followed me, and the guy driving did wear a hat like it. I wish I would have gotten a look at his face." Hope bit down on her nails.

"I don't recognize him," Charity stated.

"Lovie, see if one of your techie friends can work on the video. Girls, I think it's best if you spent the night here tonight. You did bring a bag, didn't you?"

Hope responded first. "Yes, ma'am. Mine is in the car."

"I sort of told Omar that I would meet him at his place. We had an argument earlier and need to do some talking."

Lovie said, "I'll follow you out."

"Call me to let me know you made it," Mom said.

Lovie followed me until I hit the freeway. He blew his horn. I blew mine.

"That's him. That's the man I saw coming out of Omar's place," I said out loud as I was pulling up next to Omar's car.

I sent a mass text to Mom, Hope and Lovie alerting them of my arrival to Omar's place. That way no one would feel left out.

I walked up the stairs. I was still debating on whether or not to use the spare key Omar had given me. Since he was home, I would knock. I raised my hand to knock, but stopped when I heard loud voices coming from inside of Omar's apartment. Both of the voices sounded familiar.

Knocking was no longer an option. I fumbled through my purse and located the spare key Omar had given me on a New Orleans Saints keychain. I eased the key inside of the lock and turned the knob.

This time I knew that what I was seeing was not an illusion. To my surprise, standing there arguing with Omar, alive and physically fit, was a man who looked identical to Uncle Jason.

Omar noticed me standing there first and then Uncle Jason's twin. "Charity, what are you doing here?" Omar asked.

I pointed at the man who was the spitting image of Uncle Jason. I stuttered. "Who is that?"

Omar responded, "It's my dad."

"Your dad." My eyes never left the man's.

"Charity, I was hoping we wouldn't meet like this."

Without a shadow of any doubt, I knew exactly who this man was. "Uncle Jason."

"My darling Charity. I've missed you."

I looked at Omar and then back at Uncle Jason. "You're supposed to be dead."

He held his hands up in the air. With a sinister grin on his face, he said, "The dead have risen."

I felt myself having an anxiety attack. I had to get out of there. I needed to breathe. I ran toward the front door to leave. Omar grabbed me by the waist before I could reach the door.

"I'm sorry, Charity, but I can't let you leave," Omar said.

"Let me? Omar, you have no choice." I looked him in the eyes. I placed my hand on his face. "You love me, don't you?"

Omar responded, "You already know the answer to that."

"Then show me."

"Don't listen to her. She's conniving like her mama," Uncle Jason said.

"Omar, listen to me. If you don't let me go, then I can accuse you of kidnapping. You're not trying to hold me against my will, so we're going to try this one more time. I'm going to walk out the door and you're not going to stop me."

I could see the fear in Omar's eyes. I didn't know if it was fear about losing me, or fear of what his father would do. "I love you, Charity."

"I love you too." I kissed him on the lips to reassure him.

He hugged me and whispered in my ear, "Go. I'll make sure he doesn't follow you."

I whispered in his ear, "Thank you." I kissed him again on the lips.

I rushed out the door. Omar blocked Uncle Jason from following behind me.

I don't think I exhaled until I was safely behind the wheel of my car and on the freeway.

I was too shaken to call anyone. I went straight to my parents' house.

Mom, Lovie and Hope were seated in the living room. They were surprised to see me.

"Uncle Jason's alive."

Shock filled each one of their faces.

CHAPTER 52

Hope

Did Charity say what I thought she said?

"Did y'all hear me? Uncle Jason is not dead." Charity stood in front of me and told us what had occurred. "He's the man on the video."

"Have you been drinking? Mom, Dad and Lovie saw him shot. Dead...blood running everywhere," I said.

"It's him. He didn't deny it was him. He looked at me and said, 'The dead have risen.' If you don't believe me, call Omar. Oh my God." Charity's hand went up to her mouth. She plopped down on the couch, almost sitting on me. "He's Omar's dad. I can't believe this is happening to me."

Mom placed her hand on Charity's back. "Bend over. Breathe in and out."

Lovie pulled out his phone. From his end of the conversation, he must have been talking to Omar. "Charity's over here about to have a panic attack. Is it true? Is Jason your father?" Lovie looked at his phone and then at us. "He hung up on me. I'm going over there."

Mom continued to pat Charity on the back. Charity tried to even her breathing. "Lovie, no. If you go over there, there's no telling what Jason will do."

I sat there. I was still in shock that the man who'd tried to destroy my family was alive.

"Get Mitch on the phone. Tell him to get over here right away," Mom said to Lovie.

Lovie left the room. I sat there and watched Mom comfort Charity. I felt helpless. I didn't know what to say or do.

Lovie returned. "He's on his way."

An hour later, Mitch was seated in the living room. I was now standing near the fireplace watching them all.

"I'm not going to be able to go to the police without proof that who you saw was Jason," Mitch said.

Charity stammered, "I'm not making this up. Omar can vouch for me, but he's not answering his phone."

"I'll call down to the station. Hold on," Mitch said.

Mitch dialed the number to the police station. He put his phone on speaker. "May I speak to Detective Underwood?" Mitch asked when the call was answered.

"Detective Underwood is on leave," she responded.

Charity said, "On leave? For how long?"

The receptionist responded, "I don't have that information. But if you would like to leave your name and number, I can have his partner call you back."

Mitch said, "That won't be necessary."

Mitch hung up. "Lexi, I'm sorry. Unless Omar can collaborate Charity's story, we're still at ground zero."

I used hand signals to get Charity's attention. She finally looked at me. I motioned for her to meet me in the other room. She made an excuse and left Mom sitting there with Mitch. I sent Lovie a text message. He left the room.

We were now all three standing in the foyer in front of the door.

"Charity, I don't know where Omar stays. I need you to either give me directions or drive us there."

"You're not going by yourselves," Lovie said. "I'll drive."

"Who's going to tell Mom?" Charity asked.

"You two go get in the car. I'll whisper it to her," Lovie said.

A few minutes later, we were leaving home. Lovie called himself laying down some rules. "When we get there, let me do the talking. Hope, you're real good with your cell phone. I need for you to take some pictures, do some voice recordings. Anything that we can use as proof that Uncle Jason is alive."

"I was already thinking that. That's why after Mitch said what he said, I knew we had to get out of there and go find him. Once we do that, the police will have no choice but to free Dad. You can't be on trial for a murder if the person you're accused of murdering isn't dead."

"Exactly," Lovie said.

"Omar's car is still here," Charity said.

We followed her to his apartment. She knocked on the door. No answer. "That's okay. I have a key." Charity pulled out the key and opened the door.

We searched through his small apartment but no one was in sight.

"I know where they may be. Lisa thought she saw him at this hotel." Charity told us about her lunch date with Lisa.

"That's the same hotel I ran into Omar at. Remember I told you he was acting nervous."

Lovie said, "Well, enough with talking. Let's go."

We rushed out and hopped in Lovie's SUV. Our destination was the hotel. Charity kept trying to contact Omar, but all her attempts were unsuccessful. We had to find him. He was the key to our dad's freedom.

CHAPTER 53

Omar

I saw on my phone that Charity and Lovie had called me several times. I didn't answer. I didn't know what to say.

"You need to decide whose side you're on. Mine or the Joneses," Dad said.

We were now in his hotel suite. He'd insisted I come with him when he left. He didn't trust me to come by myself so he had me ride with him. On the way over to the hotel, I contacted Jake and told him I needed to take a quick leave due to a family emergency. He wasn't too happy to hear that, but he had no choice but to accept it.

"Haven't I always been loyal?" I asked.

"Until now. How could you let Charity go? You know she was going directly to the police," he said.

"If she was going to the police, Jake would have called."

"Maybe she didn't go to the police, but letting her go was still a mistake."

"What was I supposed to do? Hold her against her will?"

I stared across the room at him.

"Until I figured out my next move."

"If you would have stayed away from my apartment like I asked you to, your cover wouldn't have been blown."

He went to the bar and poured himself a drink. "I felt like I was caged up. I got tired of being in this hotel room," he said. "A father should be able to spend time with his son."

His attempt to use the sympathy card no longer worked. I stood.

"Where were you all those times I cried myself to sleep? How about the times I called you and begged you to come get me? The only reason why you want me around is so I can help you out of this mess you've gotten yourself in."

He walked over to me and placed one hand on my shoulder. "Omar, not being there for you is one of the few regrets I have. If I could do it all over again, I would have had you come stay with me."

"But you didn't. Do you know I've been doing things for Slim?"

"That lowlife who's not worthy to even shine your shoes?" he said.

"Well, Slim and I came up on the streets together. I owed him. But the only thing with Slim, no matter what you do, you're never paid in full. You're forever in his debt."

"It's like that with crooks like him."

Dad had the nerve to talk about Slim, but he was just as slimy.

"Where's your laptop?" he asked. "I need to leave Shreveport. I thought I was going to be able to stay around to see what happened with Royce. We both need to get out of here."

"We left my apartment so quick that I didn't have a chance to pack anything," I said. "It doesn't matter, though. You can go, but I'm not going anywhere."

"My cover is blown. You can't stay. People will be asking too many questions," he said.

"I knew faking your death wasn't going to work," I said.

"It would have. But no, you couldn't keep your pants up. You got wrapped up in the Jones web, thinking she really loved you. The only thing Charity loves is money. When she realized you don't make much on a cop's salary, she would have left you regardless."

"Charity's not like what you described. Yes, she's spoiled. I can't deny it, but she's with me because she loves me, the man; not what I can do for her."

"I've been around Charity all of her life. She grew up with a silver spoon in her mouth. Royce spoiled her. He's ruined her for other men. You're not perfect and the more she spent time with you, the more she would have discovered that you aren't."

"I'm glad I no longer depend on you for my self-esteem. If I did, I would be feeling worse than I am. I'm feeling bad not because of how Charity made me feel. I feel bad because of how I've made her feel. I love her and because of you, I've betrayed her. How am I supposed to get her to trust me again?"

"Forget the trick. She's not worth it."

Before I knew it, I'd punched him. Years of frustration that was built up, along with animosity regarding his comment about Charity, were all combined in that one punch.

He stumbled to the floor. "Don't you ever lay your hands on me again. You hear me." Dad staggered while getting off the floor. He stared at me with cold, black eyes. His hand rubbed his jaw.

"I'm sorry." I was wrong for hitting my father. He'd made me so upset that I'd hit him before I realized it. "I'll go get some ice for your face."

"No time for that. We need to go back to your apartment to get your laptop."

Thirty minutes later, we were in my apartment. This time I grabbed a suitcase and threw some clothes in it and the most important things, the box full of pictures of Mom and a picture on the side of my bed of Charity. I placed the laptop in its case.

"Son, looks like you have company. I see the whole Jones clan pulling into the parking lot."

"Hit me," I say.

"I'm not going to do it," he insisted.

"I need you to hit me. Hit me hard. I need them to believe you knocked me out."

"Just don't answer the door," he said.

"Charity has a key, remember? Come on. Hurry up. You can go out the back window. There's a fire escape. Here's the laptop." I handed him the bag. "The password to access it is Mom's name."

He grabbed the bag from me. "We both need to leave."

"I can't. Go. This will buy you enough time to get away."

"Okay. You asked for it."

His arm swung back and hit me. I didn't have to pretend. I fell to the floor.

CHAPTER 54

Lovie

The trip to the hotel was unsuccessful. The hotel staff wouldn't allow us to look at the guest registry. We went knocking on every door on the seventh floor but without any results.

Charity wanted to wait for Omar back at his apartment in case he returned. I wasn't letting her go back by herself. All three of us got back in my SUV and drove straight to the hotel.

This time Charity didn't bother to knock on Omar's door. She used her key. The apartment was dark. She turned the light on. The place was a mess. It looked like there had been a struggle. Omar was laid out on the floor. Charity ran to his side. "Omar! Omar, wake up."

Omar moved his head. His eyes barely opened. "Charity, is that you?"

"Yes, baby, I'm here."

I asked, "Where's Jason?"

Charity said, "Lovie, he's hurt. Help me get him up."

"Move. I've got this." I eased my arm around him and pulled him up.

I led him to the couch. Charity rushed to his side. Hope remained quiet.

Omar rubbed his head. "My dad's looking for you, Charity. I had to stop him. I couldn't let him harm you or anyone else."

"I knew you cared," Charity said. They held each other's hands.

He might have had Charity fooled, but I didn't believe anything coming out of his mouth right then. He had a lot of explaining to do.

I stood in front of him. "Where's Jason?" I asked again.

"I don't know," Omar responded.

I bent down and removed the gun I had in my boot. I held the gun and pointed it at Omar. "Let's try this again. Where's Jason?"

Charity and Hope gasped. Charity said, "Lovie, put the gun down."

"I will as soon as he answers my question."

Hope walked over to me and placed her arm on my shoulder. "He's not worth it."

"I'm not going to shoot him." I paused. "Unless he makes me." I waved the gun back and forth. "You've got one minute. I don't plan to kill you, but if you don't answer my questions, I will make sure you will never be able to procreate." I aimed the gun directly at his crotch.

"I don't know. I don't know where my father is," he insisted.

"See, this is what I don't understand about you, Omar. You sat here and let my father get locked up for supposedly killing Jason, and all of this time, you knew he wasn't dead. And you say you love my sister." I looked at Charity when I said it.

"I do love Charity. I had nothing to do with any of this."

My forehead cringed. "That's where you're lying. Charity's confided in you. Man, I've confided in you. We all trusted you. You could have come to us at any time and shared with us that he was alive."

Omar's head fell down. He couldn't even look me in the face. "Lovie, man, I should have said something. Try to see it from my point of view. I couldn't betray my father."

My hand flew up to my forehead. I closed my eyes. "I don't give a damn about your father. My own father has been in jail suffering and you want me to feel sorry for you."

I threw the gun down on the chair and ran straight to him. I grabbed him by the collar and jerked him off the couch.

Charity said, "Lovie, don't. He's already hurting."

I felt myself foaming at the mouth. I pushed him back on the couch. "My sister's the only thing saving you." I clenched my fist. "I swear I feel like punching you in the face until I get tired."

Hope grabbed me by the arm. "Calm down, Lovie."

I needed to. My sisters had only seen me this angry once and that was when I had beaten up Tyler for messing over the both of them. What Omar did was much worse.

"He's not worth it," Hope said. "See, Charity, I told you he couldn't be trusted."

Charity's tear-stained face looked directly at us and then at him. "Omar, if you ever cared about me, tell me why you helped him."

Omar shifted his body to where he was now facing Charity. "I wanted to tell you. But Dad threatened to harm you if I did. I couldn't let that happen."

"You're a cop. You're supposed to uphold the law," Hope blurted out.

"Y'all don't understand. I haven't been able to rest because of this. I was trying to protect him. Protect y'all."

Hope's hand flew to her mouth. "Oh my God. Did you kill Mr. Franklin?"

Omar shook his head. "I swear to you that I didn't have anything to do with what happened to Mr. Franklin."

"But your dad did. Do you know he's killed several people? Several people would still be alive if you had come forth and told us you knew Jason wasn't dead."

"In Omar's defense, we don't know if Jason had anything to do with any of those other killings," Charity said.

"Charity, I can't believe you're taking up for him."

"I can," Hope said as she stood. "It's like he has her under some type of spell or something."

"I'm trying to look at things from his point of view," Charity said.

"Screw his view. All I want to know now is where is Jason?"

Omar looked me in the eyes and responded, "I honestly don't know."

"You're coming with us. I want you to look Mom in the face and tell her what you've done."

I reached for Omar. This time he blocked me.

"No need for that. I'm coming. I owe your family that."

I walked behind him to make sure he didn't try to escape. I threw Hope my keys. "You drive. Omar's sitting in the back with me."

CHAPTER 55

Lexi

I was still upset with Mitch. He was supposed to be working for Royce and me. However, he acted like he was working for the police. I called all of my kids, but none of them answered their phones. With everything going on, I did not need that type of stress.

I had promised Lovie I wouldn't drink myself into a drunken state, but I was about to go back on the promise because my nerves were bad. I needed something to calm them and I didn't smoke. The front door swung open as I was pouring myself a drink.

I turned to face the doorway. I saw my kids and Omar standing before me. "What's going on?"

Omar looked like he'd lost a fight with Mike Tyson. The right side of his face was swollen and his eyes were puffy. The top part of his shirt was torn.

Lovie spoke out first. "Omar, tell my mother what you know."

Omar looked bewildered but did as Lovie instructed. I felt my blood pressure rising while listening to Omar tell me how he knew Jason.

Hope shouted, "We don't have time for this! We need to find Jason!"

I walked up to Omar, pulled back my hand and slapped him. I didn't care that his face was swollen already. I didn't care about Charity's feelings for him. All I knew was that this man had been in my house, had been sleeping with my daughter, and my husband had been in jail for two long months because of Jason. Omar could take the easy way and cooperate with us or he could the hard way, but either way he was going to talk.

Omar rubbed the other side of his face.

"Mom, you didn't have to hit him so hard." Charity rubbed his hand and walked him to the couch.

This pissed me off even more. "He's lucky that's all I did." I was too upset to sit down so I paced back and forth in front of them.

Hope said, "We tried to get him to tell us where Jason was, but he wouldn't so Lovie decided to bring him over here."

Lovie stood in front of Omar. "Now tell my mother the fairytale story of why you didn't tell us Uncle Jason was still alive."

Omar could barely look me in the face. He kept staring at something on the wall instead of looking at me directly. This was bull. He was not going to get off this easy.

"Look at me," I said. "Look at me when you tell me why you let my husband be in jail for killing someone who isn't really dead. I said, look at me."

Omar looked up at me with big, brown, puppy dog eyes. "Mrs. Jones, I am so sorry. I never meant to hurt you or your family. My father left me no choice but to go along with what he was doing," his voice stuttered as he talked.

I wasn't buying it. "You had plenty of chances to tell us what was going on. You pretended to help us, but all along, you were plotting against us. You chose to align yourself with the likes of Jason so from this day on, consider yourself an enemy of our family."

Charity said, "Mom, let's not go that far. Let's talk about all of this later on. Right now, let's concentrate on finding Uncle Jason."

With hands on my hips and a scowl on my face, I said, "Omar, you need to tell me where Jason is now! Finding him is very important to the freedom of my husband. And if you want us to have some type of empathy when it concerns you and this situation, you will cooperate."

"Mrs. Jones, I swear to you that I don't know where he is. He knocked me out and left my apartment because I let Charity go."

"You should have an idea. Think. Think hard."

Omar lamented, "He wouldn't tell me of his plans. He was concerned that I would tell Charity."

Charity said, "Mom, if Omar was really working with his dad, he never would have let me go. He could have held me hostage, but he didn't."

I ignored Charity. I looked at Lovie. "Lovie, check his pockets for his phone. Get Jason's number off there."

Lovie did as instructed. He searched Omar's pocket and located his cell phone. Lovie looked at Omar. "What's your code? I can't access it without it."

Omar responded, "It's one nine seven five."

Lovie scrolled through Omar's phone. He said, "When the call goes through and he picks up, don't tell him you're with us. Act like you're alone."

Lovie hit the speaker button. We listened to the phone ring. When I thought it was going to voicemail, a voice asked, "Omar, are you okay?"

That really was Jason. My mouth dropped open in disbelief. I would've recognized his voice anywhere.

I wanted to say something but willed myself to remain quiet.

Omar said, "Dad, I'm fine. Where are you?"

"I'm back at the hotel. I need you to rent me another car."

"For what?" Omar asked.

"I've got to get out of town."

"Where will you be going?"

Jason responded, "It's best that you don't know. I can't risk you telling where I'm headed."

Omar said, "I'll be there as soon as I can."

"Hurry. If I know anything about those Joneses, they aren't going to give up on pestering you about my whereabouts."

The call disconnected.

Jason was correct. We weren't going to give up; especially now.

CHAPTER 56

Charity

Mom and Lovie wouldn't stop yelling at Omar. All the back-and-forth bickering made my head feel like it wanted to explode. I yelled, "Stop!"

I knew it seemed strange for me to care about Omar but I did. I couldn't let them keep harassing him the way that they were.

Everyone's eyes were on me. I looked at Mom and then at Lovie. "Can y'all give me a minute alone with Omar?"

Mom responded, "You have two minutes and then he needs to go get a car. Lovie, you will go with him and bring Jason back here. In the meantime, let me try to reach Mitch."

"Thanks, Mom," I said.

They left Omar and me alone. I really had no idea what I wanted to say. This was a messed-up situation. The man that I loved and was about to marry was the son of the man that I despised.

Omar reached for my hand, but I snatched it away. Although I took up for him in front of my family, he wasn't off the hook for what he had done.

I looked at him with disgust in my eyes. How could I have been so blind? I shook my head. All of this time, I'd been sleeping with the enemy.

Omar looked at me with those piercing brown eyes as he liked to do sometimes. Those eyes used to make me melt, but now, they had no effect on me. "Charity, I'm sorry," he said. "I regret I didn't tell you about Jason. It's a complicated situation with him being my father. It was completely selfish of me to keep the information from you. I knew if you knew who he was and who he was in relation to me, you wouldn't have anything to do with me."

"You're right. I never would have allowed you into my home, into my family circle and most importantly, into my heart."

Omar stood by me and tried to wrap his arms around me. I pushed him away.

"Don't! Do you realize how much I trusted you? Do you realize that I was taking up for you time after time when Lovie and Hope told me they didn't trust you?" I turned around in a circle. "Now here I am standing looking like a fool. They were right and I was absolutely wrong. I'm beginning to think that I can't even trust my own judgment anymore."

"Charity, I will do anything I can to make things right with you. Just name it and I will do it." I could see the fear of losing me in his eyes as he spoke.

"All I want from you right now is for you to tell the police that Jason is alive so they can release my father out of jail. You have the proof so you need to show it to them. Also while you're doing that, don't leave out the fact that he's your father and you've known all along that he was alive." I shook my head. "You don't deserve to be a policeman. You're supposed to uphold the law, but here you were helping this criminal."

"Baby, you're upset. Please calm down. Please. Please don't let this interfere with my job or us. You know how much I love you and you know how much I've always wanted to be a detective. If you take both of those things away from me, I'll have nothing."

"You should have thought of that before you set out to hurt me and my family."

"Charity, that's what I'm trying to tell you. I wasn't trying to hurt you and your family. When I first saw you, I had no idea you were a Jones. All I knew was that I needed you in my life, in my world."

I looked at him with pity in my eyes. "Omar, how do you expect us to be together after this? This is too much. I can't take this."

Omar grabbed my hand and held it. This time I didn't pull away. He looked into my eyes. "Charity, I'm going to do whatever I can to make this up to you. Promise me you will reconsider. Please. I beg you. Do not break up with me."

I looked at the ring on my finger. It was supposed to symbolize the love between the two of us. I couldn't deny my feelings but yet, I also knew that there was too much between us for us to go forward.

I started removing the ring. Before I could do so, Omar grabbed my hand. He got down on one knee. "Charity, please, baby, please don't do this."

I was having too many conflicting emotions. The sensible side of me knew that things would never ever be the same between the two of us. But my heart still loved him, still wanted to be with him, and as strange as it seemed, I wanted to be there for him throughout all of this fiasco.

I let the ring remain on my finger. He stood and wiped the tears that were flowing down my face.

Mom and Lovie returned to the room without Hope.

She said, "You two will have to talk later. Omar, we've already arranged to rent a car so it's time."

Omar squeezed my hand.

Mom continued to say to Omar, "Lovie's going to go with you. You are to convince your dad to get in the car with you. Lovie will be in the backseat. You are to bring him back here. I would go with you, but I'm waiting on a call from our attorney so we can figure out a way to get my husband home."

"I understand," Omar replied.

Lovie handed Omar a clean shirt. Omar removed the torn one and handed it to me. He put on the clean shirt and buttoned it.

"Just in case Lovie needs some backup, one of the girls will be going with you," Mom said.

Omar looked at me. "Charity, I think it's best that you stay."

"I agree," Mom said. "Charity's staying with me. Hope will be accompanying you two."

"But, Mom," I said.

She looked at me. "The decision has already been made so, Charity, deal with it."

Mom placed her arm around my shoulder as we watched them leave out from the front door. Just like Omar had aligned himself with Jason, my allegiance was with my family. I trusted my mother and whatever happened from this point on was out of our hands.

CHAPTER 57

Hope

I knew it. I knew that I was right about Omar. I knew there was something about him that could not be trusted. Charity should have listened to me. If she would have listened to me, she could have saved herself the heartache and headache of dealing with him.

We headed straight to the car rental location. We left Lovie's truck in the parking lot. Omar got in the front seat. Lovie and I both got in the backseat. Lovie pulled out his gun. Omar looked in the rearview mirror. I could tell by how his eyes bucked that he saw the gun.

Lovie handed Omar the car keys. "Let's get going."

The backseat was spacious enough for both Lovie and me to get low so we would be unnoticed. We weren't close to the hotel so we didn't try to hide yet.

Lovie said, "I hope you know that just because you're helping us out, it doesn't change anything."

I said, "I can't believe Charity's still in love with you."

Omar said, while pulling on to the highway, "You don't understand, but I promise you I will make it up to all of you."

Lovie said, "I don't want to hear your excuses. Stop talking and drive."

We rode the rest of the way in silence. Omar pulled the car into the parking lot of the hotel.

"Call him," Lovie said, as he handed Omar his phone.

"Dad, I'm outside. It's a Green SUV," Omar said.

Lovie said, "Don't forget I have this gun behind you. Don't make any sudden moves. You need to insist that you will drive. You need to drive us straight back to our house. No funny moves because I will not hesitate to shoot. Is that understood?"

Omar responded, "I'm not going to do anything. Lovie, chill with the gun. You don't want anybody to get hurt. You're simply upset right now."

"That psychology mess is not going to work on me," Lovie disclosed. "Duck, Hope. That looks like him now."

Lovie and I shifted so we were on the floor of the SUV. I heard a knock on Omar's window.

Omar said, "I'll drive. I need you to drop me off at my place."

Jason raged, "I don't have time for this. I gotta get out of here."

Omar popped the trunk. "You can put your luggage back there."

I could tell Jason wasn't happy about it because he was mumbling when he jumped in the passenger seat and closed the door.

Omar pulled off and drove onto the highway.

"You're going the wrong way," Jason said.

Lovie shifted in the backseat with his gun held high. "Hi, Uncle Jason."

"What in the hell?" Jason exclaimed.

"Don't even think about it. If you do, we'll all die tonight because I'm busting a cap in your son's head."

Jason shifted in his seat so that he and Lovie were staring at each other in the eyes.

He then looked at Omar. "I can't believe you set me up. My own son. I thought I could trust you."

Omar remarked, "Did you not notice the gun?"

Lovie and I listened as the father and son went back and forth about their current situation.

Up until now I hadn't made myself known. I was still trying to come to terms with the fact that Uncle Jason was not dead; that he was alive and that he was in the car sitting right in front of me.

Lovie said, "Omar, ignore him. Keep driving to your destination."

Uncle Jason said, "Can't believe you finally got you some balls. I guess with Royce being in jail, you had to step up and act like a man."

"I don't want to hear my father's name come out of your mouth," Lovie said.

I broke my silence and made my presence known. "How could you? How could you let him get arrested?"

Uncle Jason laughed. The kind of laugh that sent chills down my spine because it was so sinister. "My dear Hope. Why, I didn't know you were here? If I had, I would have sat in the back with you so we could cuddle."

Lovie shoved the gun to Jason's face. "You will not disrespect my sister ever again."

Jason didn't back down. "You Jones kids are something else. You've always been spoiled. You always thought you were better than everyone else. I really enjoyed watching you sweat."

With a shaken voice, I said, "Lovie, give me the gun."

Lovie glanced at me. "Hope, chill out. I've got this."

My body shook with anger. Memories of everything Uncle Jason had done to my family and me came to the forefront of my mind. Charity had to see Omar for what he was. He was the seed...the product of Jason's. Charity had to open up her eyes and see that Omar was no good. Just like his no-good daddy.

We were finally at our family home. Omar pulled into the driveway and parked right behind Charity's car.

Lovie said, "Turn the ignition off and hand me the keys."

Omar did as instructed.

Lovie said, "Omar, get out. Hope, get out. I'm getting out from your side."

I opened the back passenger door and exited the SUV. Lovie slid over, never taking his eyes or the gun off Jason. He jumped out of the backseat, then held the latch and opened the front door on the passenger side.

"Out the car now!" Lovie yelled.

Jason sat there.

Lovie said, "When you get out, if you make any funny moves, like I told Omar, I will not hesitate to shoot."

Lovie cocked his gun and Jason jumped out.

Omar now stood beside me. Lovie shoved the gun at the back of Jason as they walked up the walkway toward the house.

I said to Omar, "If you love Charity the way you claim you do, I suggest you fall back."

"Hope, get the door," Lovie instructed.

I eased past Lovie and Jason and unlocked the door. I held the door open. Lovie walked Jason to the living room. He pushed him through the door. Jason stumbled and almost fell but caught his balance.

Mom stood and came face to face with Jason. "Well, well, well. If it's not the walking dead."

CHAPTER 58

Lovie

It's a good thing that Hope was with me because I was so tempted to release the trigger and shoot Jason. I would have easily exchanged places with my father. I had so much rage built up inside of me that I needed to release it somehow. I felt like hitting something or better yet shooting something.

Mom circled around Jason as he stood there with this disgusting smirk on his face. Jason grinned at her.

I pushed him further into the room.

Mom said, "Hope, take Omar upstairs. Charity's up there. And while you're there, stay and watch and make sure he doesn't try anything. Lovie, bring this piece of trash with you. We're going to the garage."

"You heard her. Move."

"I see you're keeping the place up," Jason said.

"Did I tell you to talk?" Mom said without turning around. The garage was connected to the kitchen. She opened the door and went outside. Jason was behind her. He stopped in the doorway. Mom clapped and the light turned on.

The light revealed an empty garage with a chair sitting in the middle of it. She walked and stood near it.

"Jason, have a seat," she said.

He did as instructed. She reached on the shelf and handed me a pair of handcuffs. "If he decides to try something, restrain him," she said.

"You can't do this. This is kidnapping," Jason said.

"How is it kidnapping when everyone thinks you're dead?" I placed the handcuffs on him.

Mom paced back and forth in front of him. "Right. You're dead, remember!"

"Lexi, you're not going to get away with this."

Mom leaned down and got in his face. "I suggest you keep your comments to yourself until I decide on what I plan to do with you." She looked at me. "Come on, Lovie. Let's go."

I followed her to the door. She clapped her hands and the lights went out.

"Lexi, come back here. You can't leave me in the dark like this. There's no air circulating. It's hot in here," Jason kept saying.

We went inside and she shut the door. She went to the cabinet and found a bottle of Hennessy. I took it from her.

"No, Mom. We need your head clear. What did Mitch say?" I asked.

"He's not saying anything. I'm waiting for him to call me back."

I poured the liquor out while I talked. "Mom, I'm thinking we should take Jason in to the police station ourselves."

"According to Mitch, the fact still remains that the police found a dead body in Jason's house. They still claim to have evidence to show that Royce killed whoever the dead person is. We know it's not Jason's body now. We also know that Royce didn't kill anyone, so even with the police knowing that Jason is alive, it still won't clear Royce."

That bit of news almost knocked me off my feet. "I thought that now with Jason being alive, Dad would be free. This is ludicrous. Mitch doesn't know what he's talking about."

"I feel the same as you do. What we need to do now is find out who the body belonged to and what happened to it. The only person who knows that information is Jason."

"He's not going to talk," I said.

"Not without being persuaded. One thing I realize about Jason that he doesn't know I have figured out is the fact that he doesn't like to be in complete darkness. That's something I recall from our night of indiscretion. I was drunk but still remember how he freaked out when it appeared we were in complete darkness. He has to have some type of light on or he goes crazy. Don't you hear him in there crying out now?"

The house phone rang. Mom walked over to the other side of the kitchen and answered. She looked at me and said, "It's Mitch.

While she talked to Mitch, I opened the garage door. "You can holler as much as you want. Nobody's around but us, so save your breath."

"Lovie, if I get out of this, I'm going to kill you with my bare hands."

"Promises, promises," I said before shutting the door.

CHAPTER 59

Omar

I wished Hope would leave the room but she didn't. In fact, she stood at the door as if she was the prison guard and Charity and I were prisoners.

Charity sat on one end of the bed and I sat on the other. I eased over nearer to her.

"You can't keep ignoring me forever," I said to Charity.

"Yes, she can," Hope said.

"He wasn't talking to you," Charity said.

"But I was talking to him," Hope retorted.

"Hope, please. Can you give us a few minutes alone?" I asked.

"No. Whatever you have to say to her, you will have to say in front of me."

Fine. I would have to pretend as if Hope wasn't there.

I reached for Charity's hand. She didn't pull away so maybe it was a good sign. I raised her hand and kissed the back of it.

"Charity, it's going to be hard at first to trust me, but if we work together, we can rebuild the trust."

"Please," Hope said.

Charity said, "Hope, I really need for you to leave the room now. You're only making this situation worse."

Hope pointed at me. "He's the reason why we're in this situation in the first place."

Charity got up, walked over to Hope and whispered something in her ear. I heard Charity say, "Please, for me."

"Fine. But I will be standing right outside of the door." Hope pointed at me again. "Don't try nothing; I'm trained in karate. You might be bigger than me, but I can bring you down." She did some type of karate move that wasn't authentic at all.

Charity pushed her out the door. Her back leaned against the door and she turned and faced me.

I really didn't know what to say. My allegiance to my father had put me in the middle and it was hard seeing my way out of the mess. But I couldn't lose Charity.

"Baby, come sit by me so we can talk," I said.

"I can talk from here," she declared.

I placed one of my hands over my heart. "You know I love you."

"You know what. I actually believe that you love me, but truthfully, Omar, that's not enough. I can't trust you. I can't trust myself around you. Jason's alive and you knew it. Come on now."

"How many times do I have to say I'm sorry?" I asked.

"If you hadn't been deceitful, you wouldn't have to say it at all," Charity responded.

The truth stung. I got up and stood near her. "Look. I can't change the past. I own up to my part in this whole fiasco. He's my father. What did you expect me to do? Turn him in when I discovered he really wasn't dead."

Charity looked directly at me with her big doe-like eyes. "Yes."

"So you're telling me if the situation was reversed, that if your dad had come to you and asked you to help him, you would have turned him down and turned him in?"

Charity couldn't look me in the face. "I don't know. Maybe. Maybe not. I don't know."

"Be honest," I said.

"Fine. Yes, I probably would have done like you. I wouldn't have said anything. But it still doesn't make what you did right!"

"I understand that, baby. That's all I wanted you to see. I wanted you to see that this was an unusual situation. I really had no choice but to do what I did. Was I wrong? Absolutely. Should I have said something to you? Yes. But what would have happened?"

"My father would be free," she responded.

"Yes, maybe," I said.

"There is no maybe. If we knew Jason was still alive, Dad would not be locked up. He would be home with us now. For that I'm having a hard time forgiving you." Charity looked at me with teary eyes. "This may be the last time we'll be together," she said.

"Charity, you don't mean it."

One of her hands touched the side of my face. "I love you. That I can't deny. But I can't be with you. Not after all of this."

I fell down to the floor on my knees. I wrapped my arms around her legs. Men weren't supposed to be weak. But I wasn't concerned about my ego. I wasn't too proud to beg. Wasn't too proud for her to see me in tears.

"Charity, I don't know what I'll do without you."

She tried to push me away, but I wouldn't let go of her legs.

"If you leave me, I will die."

"Omar, no you won't. Get up. You'll be fine."

I stood near her. Charity didn't hit my hand when I used one of my hands to wipe the tears from her face. I grabbed her in my arms and kissed her. Not a gentle kiss but a passionate one. I kissed her like my life depended upon it. I wanted Charity to feel how much I loved her. I wanted her to see that our bond couldn't be broken. Yes, the circumstances were bad, but it didn't mean we had to end.

I pulled down her pants and removed them and her panties. I held her buttocks with my hands and made love to Charity with my mouth. I turned her around and she was now facing the wall. I eased inside of her from the back. I bit down on the back of her neck as I pounded into her wet flesh. We climaxed together as sweat dripped down both of our bodies.

Charity turned around and faced me. She put her clothes back on while I did the same. She bit her bottom lip. She stood in front of me and I wrapped my arms around her. Charity laid her head on my shoulder and cried. I cried along with her.

"Baby, it's going to be all right," I said, although I knew things between us would never be the same.

CHAPTER 60

Lexi

I decided to let Jason sit in the garage all night long. I stayed at the kitchen table. Lovie and I took turns keeping watch in case Jason figured out a way to slip out of the handcuffs. I had Lovie place some tape over his mouth since Jason failed to keep his mouth shut.

I rubbed the back of my sore neck. I dozed off several times at the kitchen table. Lovie had suggested for me to go get in the bed, but I refused to leave him down there by himself.

The sun peeking through the kitchen window awakened me. It was a new day and now we had to deal with the problem in the garage.

Lovie's head was down on the table. He was snoring and I really didn't want to wake him but had no choice. I gently shook his shoulder.

"What!" He shot straight up in his chair.

"Dear, we need to check on our invited houseguest," I said.

Lovie stretched and yawned. "So what do we do from here?"

"We're going to bring him back into the house. Sit him at the table and I need you to record his confession."

My plan sounded simple. Lovie left but instead of returning, I heard him yell. "Help. He's passed out."

I ran out into the garage. "Hit him," I said.

Lovie hit Jason, but he didn't wake. Lovie hit him again. He still didn't move. His head remained limp.

"Get him loose. Bring him into the house."

I ran to the stairwell and yelled out. Hope came to the top of the steps. "Mom, what's wrong?"

"It's Jason. Do you know CPR?" I asked.

"No, but I know who should," she responded. "I'll get Omar."

"Bring him to the kitchen."

I returned to the kitchen just as Lovie placed Jason on the floor.

Omar, with Charity and Hope behind him, rushed into the kitchen. "What happened?" Omar asked.

"He's not breathing is all I know," Lovie said.

"He still has a pulse," Omar said. "Move out of the way," he said to Lovie.

We stood around him as he performed CPR on Jason. One part of me wanted Jason to really be dead because of all of the problems he'd caused my family, but we needed him alive in order to save my husband, so I said a silent prayer that what Omar was doing would revive him.

I thanked God when I heard Jason cough.

"What happened?" I heard Jason say.

"Dad, you passed out," Omar said.

"It was hot in there. I told them it was too hot to be leaving me," he said as he looked around with us all staring down at him.

"Get him up," I demanded.

Lovie assisted Omar in getting Jason situated. They sat him in the chair.

"Y'all almost killed me," Jason spouted off at the mouth.

"Don't make me regret having Omar revive you," I said.

I looked at Lovie. He pulled out his cell phone and got in position.

I sat in the chair right across from Jason.

I looked at my girls and then at Omar. "I think it's best that you all leave us alone."

"We can't leave you alone with this monster," Hope said.

"Lovie will stay. Y'all go ahead. Don't let Omar leave or use the phone," I said.

Charity said, "Mom, Omar's on our side."

"Since when?" I threw my hand in the air out of frustration. "I'll deal with you and him later. Now go."

They cleared the room. "Now back to you."

Jason coughed. "Can I have some water?"

"Lovie, get the man something to drink."

Lovie went to the cabinet and got a cup and then water out of the faucet. He placed the cup in front of him.

Jason downed the water fast. "Some more, please."

"That'll be it for now. You'll get some more when you answer some of my questions," I said.

"When I get out of this, you will pay," Jason said.

I laughed. "You're talking a lot of noise for a man with very few options."

"Omar's a trained police officer. He loves me. Do you actually think he's going to let you get away with this? I know my son. He's probably planning something now."

"You may know your son, but I recognize a little bit about him too. He loves Charity. Don't like that fact, but he does. And his love for her will trump his love for you. It already has."

"Never. You'll see." Jason winked his eye.

"I was going to have Lovie give you some more water, but I don't like your attitude. Maybe I'll change my mind if you answer a few questions. Number one, whose body was that in the fire?" I asked.

"I don't know," he responded.

"You have to know. Two men brought the body and you opened up your back door and let them in. So Jason, I'm going to ask you once more, whose body was that?" I stared him in the face without blinking.

"The man was already dead when they brought him there," Jason said.

"Who? Who helped you?" I asked.

"Nobody."

"You just said 'they'...so who is 'they'?" I asked. My patience was running thin with him.

"I'm not bringing anyone else into this."

"Jason, it's too late for that. Omar's knee deep in it."

"I will tell you everything you want to know, but you have to promise me one thing," Jason said.

"Mom, don't make a deal with the devil," Lovie said.

"Let me hear him out." I looked at Jason. "I'm going to listen and then I'll decide on whether or not I will agree."

"Mom," Lovie pled.

"I've got this," I assured him.

Jason sighed. "I will make a full confession if you promise me that it will not get out that Omar assisted me."

"I can't promise you that," I replied.

"Then, my lips are sealed. I guess Royce and I might end up being cell mates."

Jason stared at me with his cold beady eyes.

"Fine. But this is the only compromise I will make. I will make sure that none of us reveal the fact that Omar helped you while you were pretending to be dead." I leaned back in my chair with my arms crossed. "It's confession time. We're waiting."

CHAPTER 61

Jason

I stared at Lexi while she talked and acted all bad, like she was the one in control, but she wasn't in control.

If me being alive could free Royce, I would be at the police station now, but there was more. They needed me and if they wanted to free Royce, they would have to give in to my demands.

I must admit that I hadn't been the best father in the world. Although I was upset at him by siding with the Joneses, Omar had been a good son to me. He had done whatever I had asked him to do. When I had asked him to have a dead body brought to my place, he made it happen. I didn't ask how, but he did.

When I told him later that I hadn't really died in the house fire, he didn't turn me into his buddies. He assisted me in any way I needed him to. The only thing he didn't do that I asked him to was stop seeing Charity. His love for her had placed me in this current situation.

I'd never told him this, but his mom was the only woman that I loved. I'd been with a lot of women over the years, but Omar's mom held a special place in my heart. I'd promised her as she lay dying in my arms that I would protect Omar. I had failed him in his teen years, so I couldn't fail him now. I would have to go to jail for faking my death. Because of my love for Omar's mom, I would make sure that he didn't go along with me.

Lexi tapped her foot under the table. "Jason, we don't have all day. I will make sure that none of us bring Omar into this, if you make a full confession."

"I don't know if I should trust you," I admitted.

"You can say what you want to about us Joneses, but not being trustworthy isn't one of them."

"You've always thought you were better than other folks. You're from the west side. You grew up right over the tracks," I said.

"Stop delaying and tell me what we need to know." Lexi faced Lovie. "Record this. I don't want there to be any misunderstanding later."

Lovie held his phone in the air.

Lexi said, "Wait, I'll be right back."

Lexi returned a few minutes later with a newspaper. She removed it from the plastic and handed it to me. She said, "Hold it up."

Lovie aimed his camera at me. He walked closer and zoomed in on the paper.

Lexi said, "State your name."

I said, "I'm Jason Milton."

Lexi instructed, "Hold the paper up. Lovie, get another good shot."

I looked up at Lovie directly into his camera and said, "I, Jason Milton, am alive as you can see. The paper I'm holding in my hands will show you today's date. I faked my death to save my life. I'd been receiving death threats from an unknown person and thought the only way to ensure my safety was to fake my death. Royce Jones was a friend of mine and had nothing to do with my death. Nor is he behind any of the death threats I'd received. I am asking that you release him as soon as possible."

Lovie stopped recording. "Who else wants you dead besides us?" Lovie asked.

"It was you, wasn't it?" I asked. A light bulb went on in my head. All of my money that went missing was because of Lovie. Had to be. He was the only person I knew smart enough to do it. No one else would have been able to figure out my account information and passwords.

Lovie smiled. "Checkmate."

I jumped out of my chair, but I was weak and fell back down. "You had no right to touch my money."

Lexi kicked me.

"Ouch," I said.

"I gave Lovie the permission to return all of the money you stole from your clients back to them. In fact, some of your clients have no idea that you stole from them. So consider yourself lucky."

"Lexi, you need to stay out of my business. That was millions of dollars. Lovie, I hope you're prepared to deal with the aftermath of what you've done."

"No, Uncle Jason. I hope you're prepared. Because as soon as you're arrested, it's going to come out how you stole money from your clients. Are you ready? Because we both know that some of your clients aren't the reputable type?"

"This wasn't part of our agreement," I said.

Lexi said, "We only agreed not to incriminate Omar along with you. We never agreed on not sharing your underhanded business practices with the police."

I wanted to reach across the table and grab Lexi around the neck and not let go until I choked her last breath from her body.

Lovie said, "And what about Mr. Franklin?"

Lexi added, "And Diana. You killed them, didn't you?"

"I'm not admitting to that. I am guilty of faking my death. That's the only thing I'm admitting to."

"That's enough. Lovie will show them the video of your confession. They'll have to do their own homework in reference to those things," Lexi said.

"So you do have a heart?" I asked.

"No. It's not about you at all. I've done enough of their work. If they want to link you to those other murders, it's up to them to do it. I'm through with it. All I want is my baby home with me."

The doorbell rang. Lexi got up. "Jason, can't say this reunion has been nice."

"Lexi, who is it?" I asked.

"We'll both see in a minute."

Two uniformed officers walked in. Hope followed behind them. One of the officers asked, "Are you Jason Milton?"

I remained quiet.

Lexi said, "Yes, that's him. That's him right there."

"Jason Milton, you are under arrest for fraud. You have the right to remain silent." The officer read me my Miranda rights.

"Lexi, this isn't over!" I yelled as they took me out in handcuffs.

CHAPTER 62

Royce

I tossed and turned on the cot. I didn't sleep well last night and couldn't sleep now.

One of the guards said, "Jones, you've got a visitor."

This wasn't one of my regular visiting days, so it must have been Mitch. I got off the bunk, slipped on my shoes and followed the guard to the private visiting room. The guard opened the door and I walked in.

My entire family and Mitch were standing inside, catching me off guard.

"What's going on here?" I asked.

Lexi ran over to me and wrapped her arm around my neck. My hand automatically wrapped itself around her. "Baby, you're coming home."

I blinked my eyes a few times and when I opened them, they were all still standing there. I wasn't dreaming. This was real. "Mitch, is this true?"

"Royce, you're a free man. We're just waiting on the warden to finish with your release papers."

Tears that I'd been holding back for the last two months flowed down my face. Each one of my kids came over to me and hugged me. Lexi stood by my side with a smile on her face.

Lovie reached from behind the table. "Thought you could use this."

Lexi said, "It's one of your favorite suits."

"Are they going to allow me to take this?" I asked Mitch.

"The guard's aware that you're being released."

"I've got a few things I have in my cell that I want to get and I'll be right back," I said.

I felt like the weight of the world had been lifted off my shoulders. The smile on my face reached from ear to ear.

The guard said, "Jones, I heard you got your walking papers."

"Yes, indeed. I'm about to clean out my cell and I'll change in there."

In less than fifteen minutes, I was dressed and had the few items I wanted to take with me in a bag and back near the visiting station. The guard looked at me and said, "I knew you were innocent."

"I did too, but didn't know if I would ever see my freedom," I admitted.

"You're a good man." The guard shook my hand. "Here are your papers. You're free to go."

I took the papers and walked into the room. "Let's go. I've got them." I waved the papers in the air.

Mitch opened the door. Lexi and I walked down the long hall, hand in hand.

We walked out of the front door. I stopped and closed my eyes. I said a quick prayer. I inhaled the fresh air. We stepped around the corner into flashing lights. Cameras were flashing and reporters with microphones were walking over to us. Mitch walked around me and tried to push them away.

"Mr. Jones, how does it feel to be a free man?" one reporter asked.

They blurted out question after question. We walked to Lovie's SUV. Lovie opened my door. Lexi got inside first and then I got in. Hope went to the other back passenger door and slipped in beside Lexi. Charity sat up front with Lovie.

Lovie had to blow his horn in order for some of the reporters to move out of the way.

"I didn't expect a media circus," I said, once we were safely off the premises.

"Neither did I," Lexi said as she squeezed my hand. "You know they will be wanting a statement."

"They can wait. I'm with my family. I've been waiting for this moment for two months now."

"Dad, you've lost weight, but the suit still looks good on you," Hope said.

Lexi fixed the handkerchief in my suit pocket. "He looks twenty years younger. I might have to get some plastic surgery because you're looking younger than me," Lexi teased.

"Baby, I could never look as good as you."

We kissed.

Hope said, "Ugh, can you at least wait until you're home and out of our eyesight?"

We stopped kissing. Lexi said, "Girl, hush."

We both laughed. It felt good to hear their laughter.

"With all of the excitement, I didn't ask why or how this all happened," I said.

"I thought Mitch told you," Lexi said.

"No, he hasn't told me anything."

Lexi said, "Jason's alive. Can you believe it? He's alive."

"Alive. How is that possible? We saw the body. We saw the fire."

I listened to Lexi and each one of my children tell me their view of what had occurred within the last twenty-four hours.

"If I saw Jason now, the police would have a legitimate reason to arrest me this time, because I would kill him. Where is he now?"

"He's been arrested for faking his death. Don't know what else is going to happen with him, but don't care because I got my baby back."

Lexi reached over and kissed me on the cheek.

Lovie could barely get down our street for some news vans. He eased his SUV through the crowd and pulled into the driveway. We rushed inside to avoid them.

"Home, sweet home," I yelled out once inside. I walked through the house as if it were my first time there.

The family gave me the space I needed. I walked to the living room and stood in the doorway. I looked at Lexi sitting in her usual spot. I noticed the girls and Lovie seated in their spots and my chair, it was empty. Waiting on me to fill it. You only miss the little things when they are no longer around. Material things come and go. Those weren't the things I missed. I missed my family. I missed being home. Home to me wasn't a two-story house; home was being around the people I loved.

CHAPTER 63

Charity

Our family reunion was a day of rejoicing. Omar had called me a few times, but I ignored his calls. After eating the meal our mother had cooked, we were now all seated in the living room in what we considered our normal seats.

"Dad, there's something I need to tell you," I said.

The phone rang, interrupting me. Lovie answered. "Dad, it's for you. It's Uncle Jason."

Our mom said, "Tell Jason to go to hell."

"Lexi, baby, it's okay. I'll talk to him, but put it on speaker."

Lovie hit the speaker button on the cordless phone.

"Hello," Jason said from the other end.

"Well, hello, Jason," Dad said.

"Royce, I hope you know the sacrifice I made for your freedom," Jason said.

"I wish you would have stayed dead and saved us all the trouble of having to deal with you."

Jason laughed from the other end. "Oh, you don't mean it. You know you miss me, old friend."

"Like a wart. Now what's the real reason for this call?"

"I wanted to say I'm sorry."

I think him saying that shocked all of us.

"You're sorry all right," Mom said. "You're a sorry piece of—"

"Lexi, let the man talk," Dad said.

"See, Royce, that's your problem. You're too forgiving. Not me."

Mom folded her arms and then crossed her legs.

"Lexi, you should be more like Royce. Forgiveness is good for the soul," Jason said.

Dad said, "Don't ever address my wife again. I will forgive you, not because I believe you're sincere with your apology, but because I need to be able to so I can move on. And Jason, I'm moving on. From this day forward, don't ever contact me, or any of my family, again. May you get what you deserve."

"Royce, don't be like that. We're brothers, remember. Friends for life."

"Lovie, hang the phone up," Dad said.

Lovie did as instructed.

"I'm glad Jason is finally out of our lives," Hope said.

Mom said, "Too bad he's still alive."

"Lexi, that's not nice," Dad said.

"I'm only saying what y'all are thinking."

"Lord, forgive us all," Dad said.

I eased out of the room and dialed Omar's number. "Where are you?" I asked.

"At home."

"Feel like some company?"

"But your dad. It's his first night home. Thought you would be staying there."

"Oh, I'm sure he and Mom would like some alone time. I don't want to hear their private reunion."

"Sure then. You know how to find me."

Two hours later, I was knocking on Omar's door. He greeted me at the door. "You could have used your key," he said as he moved to the side and allowed me in.

"What's all of this? Boxes and things." I noticed quite a few boxes packed or empty.

"I made a few phone calls today."

I followed him into his bedroom. There were clothes in suitcases on the bed.

He went on to say, "I accepted a job in Dallas."

I was stunned. "I never knew you were looking to move to Dallas."

"I applied for the job a year ago. They offered it to me right around the time I made detective here."

"So what about us?" I asked. "Were you going to leave without telling me?"

"I was hoping that you would come with me. Out there nobody knows you or me. We could start our lives over together. Just you and me."

"Omar, I can't just up and leave my family like that. I love you but what you're asking is too much. If you stay, maybe we can work things out."

Omar sat on the bed and then pulled me down on his lap. "So if I stay, can you promise me that you and I will work past all of this and be together?"

I couldn't do it and refused to lie to him that I would be able to. "Truthfully, I don't know. I can try. But I don't know what's going to happen tomorrow. Right now, I'm here. That should be enough."

"That's just it. You're here now. But what about when your mom, your brother or sister, or especially your dad, says something about me? How supportive will you be then?"

"You put your own self in this situation. If you would have been honest with me, we wouldn't be having any issues."

"And I wouldn't have you, either," he noted.

"I love you, Omar. It's something that I can't deny. But I can't forget about my life here. I have a thriving business. Dad's home now. I can't move to Dallas."

I saw a tear fall from Omar's eyes. "I wish you would change your mind."

"I can visit you," I said.

"You might for a while, but eventually the visits will stop. You will stop calling or answering my texts. If we're going to make a clean break, I guess we need to start now."

I kissed the lone tear from his face. My lips landed on top of his. He moved the suitcases off the bed and we made love the last time as if it were our first time. We explored one another's bodies and climaxed in unison.

He walked me to the door afterward. "I guess this is good-bye," I said.

"I can't bring myself to say those words," he confessed.

I kissed him one last time. I walked out his front door and got inside of my car. Once inside, I cried like a baby. Cried because once again, a man I loved had betrayed me. Once betrayal entered into the picture, it was hard turning back. Our love was fine for a moment in time, but it wasn't strong enough to stand in the aftermath of what had transpired between our fathers.

CHAPTER 64

Lexi

It'd now been a month since Royce's release from jail. Life as the Joneses once knew it had changed. We were at our new norm. I vowed never to take my life or my family for granted again.

Things that were once important to me, such as my status in the community or having the newest car or being considered the best dressed whenever I entered a room, no longer mattered to me. Don't get me wrong; having those things were nice, but they were no longer at the forefront of my mind or occupied my thoughts during the day as they had once done prior to Royce's arrest.

I walked into the dining room carrying my homemade peach cobbler. The crust was crisp and the peaches sweet. "Who's ready for dessert?"

I scooped out cobbler and placed it on everyone's plate. Royce took the Tupperware dish and placed it near him. "Have a seat. You've been on your feet most of the day cooking," he said.

"No complaints here," I said. "Seeing your smiling faces and hearing those forks hit the plate were all the thanks I needed."

"Mom, you outdid yourself with this cobbler," Lovie said.

"Just when I said I was going on a diet, you cook my favorite," Hope said.

"Girl, please. You do not need to lose any weight," Charity said. "Now, me. It seems like *I've* gained a few pounds."

"Yes, you do look a little thick," I said. "I hope it's just fat and nothing else.

"No, Mom. It's just fat. I confirmed it."

Good, I thought. When Charity told us that Omar had relocated to Dallas, I wanted to throw confetti in the air. I was relieved to learn that she wasn't pregnant by him because I hoped, with distance, their interaction with one another would fizzle.

"Hope, I thought Raymond was going to come by with you today," I said.

"Lovie intimidates him," Hope said.

Lovie pretended to ignore her.

Royce said, "Who is this Raymond I keep hearing about?"

"Nobody special," Lovie responded.

"You're just mad because his brother used to beat you in basketball."

"So he says," Lovie said in between bites.

"Tell Raymond if he's going to be dating my baby girl, that I need to meet him," Royce said.

I agreed. "Yes. He must be thoroughly checked out."

"I suggest you run a background check on him too," Charity added.

"I'm already on it," Lovie said.

"Y'all know we went to high school together," Hope said.

"But what happened after high school? I'll have a report back tomorrow," Lovie said.

"Mom, tell him it's not necessary."

"I'm all for it. Royce, what do you think?"

"I'm from the old school, but with the way things are now, Lovie has my blessings. Check this Raymond out. If he checks out, then I will meet him."

Hope pouted. "Y'all are going overboard."

"Better safe than sorry. Trust me," Charity said.

"How are things down at the funeral home?" I asked Royce.

"Thanks to my son, everything is running smoothly. He did a good job stepping in during my absence."

"Thanks, Dad," Lovie said.

"I mean it. We've bumped heads a lot in the past, but I wanted you to know that I understand you're your own man. I've been thinking. There's a section of space on the other side of the funeral home that's not being used. If you like, we can get it remodeled. You can use it for an office space and start your own accounting firm. Well, make it official."

"Royce, that's a great idea. What do you say, Lovie? Isn't it a great idea?"

I crossed my fingers and hoped that Lovie would agree. He didn't say anything at first. I hoped there would be no friction.

Lovie responded, "I'm all for it. This is perfect timing. I'm trying to transition my clients to someone else now. I'd put in some applications at a few firms, but now I can put it on the back burner."

"Push it right out of your mind. I have a selfish reason for doing it. I want you to still continue to be our accountant and I'm hoping that if and when I do decide to retire, you will take over the family business."

"Dad, I will honestly consider it."

"It's good seeing my two favorite men getting along," I said.

Royce stood. "I have an announcement to make. As you well know, Lexi and I had planned on renewing our vows on our thirtieth wedding anniversary. Well, instead of a big party, we have decided to celebrate by taking a seven-day cruise."

"That's going to be nice." Charity frowned. "But we wanted to celebrate with you."

"And you can. Because..." Royce pulled out three envelopes from his pocket. "You three are coming along with us."

They were all excited. In all of our travels, this would be our first cruise.

"I can't wait," Hope said. "That means we need to go shopping." She looked at Royce. "We can go shopping for some new clothes for the trip, can't we?"

All of us except Lovie looked at Royce. "Yes, but I will have to give you ladies a limit. Don't want you spending all of your money before we get on the ship."

"Thank you, Daddy," Hope said.

Hope ran up to Royce and kissed him on the cheek.

Later that night, Royce and I were alone, relaxing on the patio enjoying the summer breeze. We lay together in the hammock like we used to do when we first bought the house. We were both looking upward at the sky.

He said, "When I was locked up, I dreamed of moments like this. Just you and me, relaxing, gazing up at the sky looking at the stars."

"There's no other place I would rather be," I said, with love in my heart and on my mind.

"I love you, Lexi," he said.

"I love you too." I placed my head on his chest and closed my eyes.

Our heart rhythms were in sync as I drifted to a peaceful state of mind. I no longer lived for drama. Our social status no longer mattered to me. As long as I had my family, all was well in my world. I hoped this quiet serene night was the prelude to a drama-free life for the Joneses.

ABOUT THE AUTHOR

Shelia M. Goss is a screenwriter and the *Essence* magazine and *Dallas Morning News* bestselling author of over twenty contemporary fiction novels, including *The Joneses, Secret Relations, Secret Liaisons, Delilah, Ruthless, My Invisible Husband, The Commitment Plan, Savannah's Curse,* and *Montana's Way*. Shelia's received many accolades for her books over the years, including being a 2012 and 2014 Emma Awards Finalist. The *Library Journal* named *The Joneses* as one of the best books of 2014. A speaker at literary conferences across the country, Shelia also works closely with librarians supporting literacy and increasing awareness via workshops for adults and teens.

You can learn more about Shelia at:

Website: www.sheliagoss.com

Facebook: www.facebook.com/shelia.goss

Twitter: http://www.twitter.com/sheliamgoss